DATE DUE

MAR 1985		
JUL 15 1985	JUN1 3 1990	
OCT 25 1985		
FEB -8 1986		
	DEC 2 6 1990	
JUL 1 2 1986	FEB 2 1 1991	
	APR 2 6 1992	
JUN 23 1987		
OCT 15 1987	AUG 1 6 1994	
MAR 24 1988	OCT 31 1997	
JUN 2 1988	MAR 2 7 2000	
OCT 20 1988	NOV 1 1 2000	
APR 2 1989	JAN 3 1 2001	
	FEB 2 - 2006	
	AUG 1 8 2006	

DEMCO

THE POETRY TROUPE

An Anthology of Poems to Read Aloud

Compiled by
ISABEL WILNER

DECORATIONS BY ISABEL WILNER

CHARLES SCRIBNER'S SONS • NEW YORK

Copyright © 1977 Isabel Wilner

Library of Congress Cataloging in Publication Data
Main entry under title: The poetry troupe.
    1. Children's poetry.   I. Wilner, Isabel.   PN6110.C4P55
    808.81   77-9439   ISBN 0-684-15198-7

1 3 5 7 9 11 13 15 17 19 M/C 20 18 16 14 12 10 8 6 4 2

Printed in the United States of America

Acknowledgments

The compiler and the publishers gratefully acknowledge the following poets, publishers, and agents for permission to reprint poems in this anthology. Every effort has been made to locate all persons having any rights or interests in the material published here. If some acknowledgments have not been made, their omission is unintentional and is regretted.

"Money" by Richard Armour. From *For Partly Proud Parents*. Reprinted by permission of the author.

"Jill Withers Had a Farthingale" by John Becker. From *New Feathers for the Old Goose* (1956) by John Becker. Reprinted by permission of Florence Feiler on behalf of the author.

"Almost," "Circles," and "Spring" by Harry Behn. From *The Little Hill*, copyright 1949 by Harry Behn; renewed 1977 by Alice L. Behn. Reprinted by permission of Harcourt Brace Jovanovich, Inc.

"Jim" by Hilaire Belloc. From *Cautionary Verses* by Hilaire Belloc. Published 1941 by Alfred A. Knopf, Inc. Reprinted by permission of Alfred A. Knopf, Inc., and the U.K. publisher, Gerald Duckworth & Co. Ltd.

"Peregrine White and Virginia Dare" by Rosemary and Stephen Vincent Benét. From *A Book of Americans* by Rosemary and Stephen Vincent Benét. Holt, Rinehart & Winston, Inc. Copyright 1933 by Stephen Vincent Benét; copyright renewed © 1961 by Rosemary Carr Benét. Reprinted by permission of Brandt & Brandt.

"Row, Row, Row," "Three Little Guinea Pigs," and "Two Cats" by N. M. Bodecker. From *It's Raining Said John Twaining* by N. M. Bodecker (a Margaret K. McElderry Book). Copyright © 1973 by N. M. Bodecker. Used by permission of Atheneum Publishers.

Contents

For Mother
and for the Poetry Troupes

Explanation

Libraries and classrooms have their own rhythms. Interests wax and wane. Today's delights may fade for a while, and reappear tomorrow. Then again they may stay around, as our poetry troupe is staying. It has held its own in our library for the past four years, with no signs of diminishing enthusiasm.

How did the poetry troupe begin? Unexpectedly, and from a number of influences, the most obvious being the informal reading together that we do in our library. This pursuit has set me to searching for narrative rhymes and poems that are conversations, especially those with refrains or choruses, that invite a child into the reading as a participant as well as a listener. Our troupe was probably taking form long before we realized it. Occasionally a teacher in the library with the children would extemporaneously play aloud with lines or verses from a poem; then teacher and librarian would recite antiphonally. I remember now a child saying, "I love it when you and Mr. G. toss those poems back and forth." Another beginning point may have come when I asked a child or two to join me in reading poetry. A few children responded by wanting to read with me every week. Small groups began to find extra minutes to come to the library and read favorite poems.

Those were influences, of course, but the idea of a troupe came from a chance to perform publicly. Even then we didn't know that we were on our way to the formation of a poetry troupe.

It happened by accident. Our position as an elementary school on a college campus makes for a rewarding relationship with college students and teachers. One fall morning when the library was full of children, a college teacher came rushing in with a sudden request. She wanted me to come to the classroom across the hall and read poems to her ten o'clock college class. While I was wondering how I'd ever get the time in the next busy twenty-five minutes to locate the poems, I looked around the library and saw several children who had frequently read with me the year before. I asked them if they'd like to go with me to read to a college class. They were delighted.

We selected five or six poems we had often enjoyed, including Harold Monro's "Overheard on a Saltmarsh," Vachel Lindsay's "The Mysterious Cat," and David McCord's "I'd Like You to Meet." We went to the class. We read. Both the children and the college students were enchanted. We returned to the library elated. Wouldn't it be fun if we could read to another college class! We hoped someone else would invite us. "Yes," said one of the children, "we'd be like the mime troupe." She was referring to a group of college students who occasionally came to the classrooms and did pantomimes for the children. "We'd be the poem troupe!" she finished. And so it was.

A week later I was taking five children across the campus to read to a college class. The word spread. Children appeared at the library asking to be in the poetry troupe, children who were constant readers, and children who hardly read at all.

One troupe was not enough. We soon had another and another. I decided that six children was the maximum number for a troupe. That made for variety, and no one had to wait too long for a turn. Our programs were short enough to make us welcome. Ten or fifteen minutes was about the right length.

A troupe is a group that goes to read, and its membership varies. Sometimes all are from one classroom; sometimes we have a mixture of ages. Last fall I took two seven-year-olds, two eight-year-olds, and two twelve-year-olds to a college class. The seven-year-olds were so enchanted with twelve-year-old Robin's reading of Valerie Worth's

"Clock," which he did with a very definite emphasis of the tick-tock rhythm, that they came back to the library eager to find the same poem and to read it in the same way.

I have been amazed at the poetry children have uncovered. Eleven-year-old Lisa was fascinated by William Blake's "A Poison Tree," but remarked under her breath, "It scares me." Seven-year-old Rachel discovered "Early One Morning" in that thick, rich volume by Geoffrey Grigson, *The Cherry Tree*. She especially liked "the deceive-me part." College students were startled to hear her say, with a combination of despair and delight:

"Oh, don't deceive me. Oh, never leave me.
How could you use a poor maiden so?"

I was surprised that ten-year-old David had learned much of the Farjeons' *Kings and Queens* during the previous year when his sister had the book from the library. In our troupe no one sets out to memorize, but children suddenly announce, "I don't need the book for that one."

Families get involved, too. Fathers and mothers contribute rhymes from their childhood, and the children bring them back on the tips of their tongues. Older brothers and sisters remember, and send the younger ones searching for half-recalled lines.

Searching for new poems is part of the fun. Everyone pores over the books. We try the poems on each other. Maybe we like them; maybe we don't. Some we accept, others we reject. The idea is to find a poem you really want to read. Partners are chosen. It may be one person for this poem, another one for that. One poem may require three or four readers, another five or six. We practice. Here is where an adult can suggest, "Why not try it this way?" or "Could each person read two lines instead of one?" We try it. Sometimes we all realize that the first way was better. Sometimes the children arrive at the best way of all.

Adults reading with children can help set the rhythmic pattern, can quickly see the voices in the poem. As for the children, they become instant participants. Rhythm and rhyme seem to push the reader forward. The give and take of the conversational poems, the variation in repetition, the joining together in creating choruses, the antiphonal reading of a long poem, all entice the reader into the poem and make reading pleasurable.

Being on a college campus has been helpful to the development of our poetry troupes. Many classes have given us a standing invitation for a ten-minute "program" whenever we're ready. But it is by no means necessary to be on a campus. There are many potential audiences. Children can share with other classrooms, or with their own class. Or they can just experience the fun of reading poetry themselves when two or three are gathered together.

I recently went to another school to tell stories and took my poetry folders, containing typed copies of some of our favorite poems. After a story, I asked if anyone would like to help me read. Hands went flying up. I picked poems with a number of characters: "Five Little Chickens," "The Sad Sliced Onion," "The Secret Song." We read, to the delight of both readers and listeners. I was told afterward that teachers rejoiced to see that many of the volunteers were by no means those known as the best readers. But here was reading as a source of joy.

Joy is the propelling force. We have found much to revel in: the play of rhyme, the bounce of rhythm, the humor of words. We have found much to savor: the ordinary, the obvious, the strange, the ominous, a poem's mysterious undertones or overtones, even the sense of something that can't be captured or understood. And we have enjoyed a situation which makes use of our initiative and gives us an opportunity to work with our friends and provide pleasure for our listeners.

Here are some of the poems we like to say, and other people like to hear.

—ISABEL WILNER

Conversations

Did You Feed My Cow?

"Did you feed my cow?"
    "Yes, Mam!"
"Will you tell me how?"
    "Yes, Mam!"
"Oh, what did you give her?"
    "Corn an' hay."
"Oh, what did you give her?"
    "Corn an' hay."

"Did you milk her good?"
    "Yes, Mam!"
"Did you do like you should?"
    "Yes, Mam!"
"Oh, how did you milk her?"
    "Swish! Swish! Swish!"
"Oh, how did you milk her?"
    "Swish! Swish! Swish!"

"Did that cow die?"
    "Yes, Mam!"
"With a pain in her eye?"
    "Yes, Mam!"
"Oh, how did she die?"
    "Uh! Uh! Uh!"
"Oh, how did she die?"
    "Uh! Uh! Uh!"

"Did the buzzards come?"
"Yes, Mam!"
"For to pick her bone?"
"Yes, Mam!"
"Oh, how did they come?"
"Flop! Flop! Flop!"
"Oh, how did they come?"
"Flop! Flop! Flop!"

TRADITIONAL

Overheard on a Saltmarsh

Nymph, nymph, what are your beads?

Green glass, goblin. Why do you stare at them?

Give them me.

No.

Give them me. Give them me.

No.

Then I will howl all night in the reeds,
Lie in the mud and howl for them.

Goblin, why do you love them so?

They are better than stars or water,
Better than voices of winds that sing,
Better than any man's fair daughter,
Your green glass beads on a silver ring.

Hush, I stole them out of the moon.

Give me your beads, I desire them.

                                No.

I will howl in a deep lagoon
For your green glass beads, I love them so.
Give them me. Give them.

                    No.

                            HAROLD MONRO

Ferry Me Across the Water

"Ferry me across the water,
     Do, boatman, do."
"If you've a penny in your purse
     I'll ferry you."

"I have a penny in my purse,
     And my eyes are blue;
So ferry me across the water,
     Do, boatman, do!"

"Step into my ferry-boat,
     Be they black or blue,
And for the penny in your purse
     I'll ferry you."

CHRISTINA ROSSETTI

Said the monkey to the owl,
"What will you have to drink?"
"Well, since you're so very kind,
I'll take a bottle of ink."

FOLK RHYME

19

Stork, Stork

Stork, stork
With a pointed bill,
Whence do you come?
From the Great Black Hill.

Stork, stork,
What do you bring?
A packet of soap
Tied up with a string.

Stork, stork,
For whom might it be?
For the mother of Aram
And Vartemi.

Stork, stork,
What will she do?
She will wash her apron
And kerchief too.

And Vartemi
Will dance and sing
Because the stork
Has come back with the spring.

ROSE FYLEMAN

Green Candles

"There's someone at the door," said the gold candlestick:
"Let her in quick, let her in quick!"
"There is a small hand groping at the handle.
Why don't you turn it?" asked the green candle.

"Don't go, don't go," said the Hepplewhite chair,
"Lest you find a strange lady there."
"Yes, stay where you are," whispered the white wall:
"There is nobody there at all."

"I know her little foot," gray carpet said:
"Who but I should know her light tread?"
"She shall come in," answered the open door,
"And not," said the room, "go out any more."

HUMBERT WOLFE

Who comes here?
A grenadier.
What do you want?
A pot of beer.
Where is your money?
I have none.
Then grenadier
Get you gone.

MOTHER GOOSE

21

The Flattered Flying Fish

Said the Shark to the Flying Fish over the phone:
"Will you join me tonight? I am dining alone.
Let me order a nice little dinner for two!
And come as you are, in your shimmering blue."

Said the Flying Fish: "Fancy remembering me,
And the dress that I wore at the Porpoises' tea!"
"How could I forget?" said the Shark in his guile:
"I expect you at eight!" and rang off with a smile.

She has powdered her nose; she has put on her things;
She is off with one flap of her luminous wings.
O little one, lovely, light-hearted and vain,
The Moon will not shine on your beauty again!

E. V. RIEU

Little girl, little girl, where have you been?
Gathering roses to give to the Queen.
Little girl, little girl, what gave she you?
She gave me a diamond as big as my shoe.

MOTHER GOOSE

The Secret Song

Who saw the petals
    drop from the rose?
I, said the spider,
But nobody knows.

Who saw the sunset
    flash on a bird?
I, said the fish,
But nobody heard.

Who saw the fog
    come over the sea?
I, said the sea pigeon,
Only me.

Who saw the first
    green light of the sun?
I, said the night owl,
The only one.

Who saw the moss
    creep over the stone?
I, said the grey fox,
All alone.

MARGARET WISE BROWN

Jam

"Spread," said Toast to Butter,
And Butter spread.
"That's better, Butter,"
Toast said.

"Jam," said Butter to Toast.
"Where are you, Jam,
When we need you most?"
Jam: "Here I am,

Strawberry, trickly and sweet.
How are you, Spoon?"
"I'm helping somebody eat,
I think, pretty soon."

DAVID MCCORD

What is the rhyme for porringer?
The King he had a daughter fair.
And gave the Prince of Orange her.

MOTHER GOOSE

24

There Was a Lady Loved a Swine

There was a lady loved a swine.
"Honey!" said she;
"Pig-hog, wilt thou be mine?"
"Hunc!" said he.

"I'll build thee a silver sty,
Honey," said she;
"And in it thou shalt lie!"
"Hunc!" said he.

"Pinned with a silver pin,
Honey," said she;
"That thou mayest go out and in,"
"Hunc!" said he.

"Will thou have me now,
Honey," said she;
"Speak, or my heart will break,"
"Hunc!" said he.

MOTHER GOOSE

The Sad Sliced Onion

Once there was an onion.
The cook sliced it
And the cook began to cry
Boo! Hoo! Hoo!

The mother came to comfort the cook
And as she leaned over the sliced onion
The tears splashed from her eyes
Drip! Drip! Drip!

Then the father arrived
To comfort the mother
And he began to cry
Mrump! Mrump! Mrump!

The little boy came to comfort the father
And when he came near the onion
Tears rolled down his checks
Wah! Wah! Wah!

And they all cried
Boo! Hoo! Hoo!
Drip! Drip! Drip!
Mrump! Mrump!
Waaaaaaaaaaaaaah!
All over an onion.

MARGARET WISE BROWN

Five Little Chickens

Said the first little chicken,
  With a queer little squirm,
"I wish I could find
  A fat little worm."

Said the next little chicken,
  With an odd little shrug,
"I wish I could find
  A fat little bug."

Said the third little chicken,
  With a sharp little squeal,
"I wish I could find
  Some nice yellow meal."

Said the fourth little chicken,
  With a small sigh of grief,
"I wish I could find
  A little green leaf."

Said the fifth little chicken,
  With a faint little moan,
"I wish I could find
  A wee gravel stone."

Said the old mother hen
  From the green garden patch
"If you want any breakfast,
  Just come here and scratch."

ANONYMOUS

Momotara

Where did Momotara go,
With a hoity-toity-tighty?
He went to lay the giants low,
The wicked ones and mighty.

What did Momotara take?
His monkey, dog and pheasant,
Some dumplings and an almond cake,
Which made the journey pleasant.

How did Momotara fare
Upon the fearful meeting?
He seized the giants by the hair
And gave them all a beating.

What did Momotara bring?
Oh, more than you could measure:
A silver coat, a golden ring
And a waggon-load of treasure.

What did Momotara do?
He sat himself astride it;
The monkey pushed, the pheasant drew
And the little dog ran beside it.

ROSE FYLEMAN

What's in There?

What's in there?
Gold and money.
Where's my share of it?
The mousie ran away with it.
Where's the mousie?
In her housie.
Where's her housie?
In the wood.
Where's the wood?
The fire burnt it.
Where's the fire?
The water quenched it.
Where's the water?
The brown bull drank it.
Where's the brown bull?
Back of the hill.
Where's the hill?
All clad with snow.
Where's the snow?
The sun melted it.
Where's the sun?
High, high up in the air!

SCOTTISH NURSERY RHYME

You Are Old, Father William

"You are old, Father William," the young man said,
   "And your hair has become very white;
And yet you incessantly stand on your head—
   Do you think, at your age, it is right?"

"In my youth," Father William replied to his son,
   "I feared it might injure the brain;
But, now that I'm perfectly sure I have none,
   Why, I do it again and again."

"You are old," said the youth, "as I mentioned before,
   And have grown most uncommonly fat;
Yet you turned a back-somersault in at the door—
   Pray, what is the reason of that?"

"In my youth," said the sage, as he shook his grey locks,
   "I kept all my limbs very supple
By the use of this ointment—one shilling the box—
   Allow me to sell you a couple?"

"You are old," said the youth, "and your jaws are too weak
   For anything tougher than suet;
Yet you finished the goose, with the bones and the beak—
   Pray, how did you manage to do it?"

"In my youth," said his father, "I took to the law,
   And argued each case with my wife;
And the muscular strength, which it gave to my jaw,
   Has lasted the rest of my life."

"You are old," said the youth, " one would hardly suppose
    That your eye was as steady as ever;
Yet you balanced an eel on the end of your nose—
    What made you so awfully clever?"

"I have answered three questions, and that is enough,"
    Said his father. "Don't give yourself airs!
Do you think I can listen all day to such stuff?
    Be off, or I'll kick you down-stairs!"

                    LEWIS CARROLL

"Mother, may I take a swim?"
"Yes, my darling daughter,
But hang your clothes on a hickory limb,
And don't go near the water."

        FOLK RHYME

"Father, may I go to war?"
"Yes you may, my son,
But wear your woolen underwear,
And don't shoot off your gun."

        FOLK RHYME

31

O sailor, come ashore,
    What have you brought for me?
Red coral, white coral,
    Coral from the sea.

I did not dig it from the ground,
    Nor pluck it from a tree;
Feeble insects made it
    In the stormy sea.

CHRISTINA ROSSETTI

Brother and Sister

"Sister, sister, go to bed!
Go and rest your weary head."
Thus the prudent brother said.

"Do you want a battered hide,
Or scratches to your face applied?"
Thus his sister calm replied.

"Sister, do not raise my wrath.
I'd make you into mutton broth
As easily as kill a moth!"

The sister raised her beaming eye
And looked on him indignantly
And sternly answered, "Only try!"

Off to the cook he quickly ran.
"Dear Cook, please lend a frying-pan
To me as quickly as you can."

"And wherefore should I lend it you?"
"The reason, Cook, is plain to view.
I wish to make an Irish stew."

"What meat is in that stew to go?"
"My sister'll be the contents!"
                              "Oh!"
"You'll lend the pan to me, Cook?"
                              "No!"
Moral: Never stew your sister.

LEWIS CARROLL

Dilly Dilly Piccalilli
Tell me something very silly:
There was a chap his name was Bert
He ate the buttons off his shirt.

CLYDE WATSON

What Is Pink?

What is pink? a rose is pink
By the fountain's brink.
What is red? a poppy's red
In its barley bed.
What is blue? the sky is blue
Where the clouds float thro'.
What is white? a swan is white
Sailing in the light.
What is yellow? pears are yellow,
Rich and ripe and mellow.
What is green? the grass is green,
With small flowers between.
What is violet? clouds are violet
In the summer twilight.
What is orange? why, an orange,
Just an orange!

CHRISTINA ROSSETTI

Little boy, little boy,
Who made your britches?
Daddy cut them out
And Mammy sewed the stitches.

FOLK RHYME

Mister Rabbit

Mister Rabbit, Mister Rabbit,
Your ears are mighty long.
Yes, my friend,
They're put on wrong!

Mister Rabbit, Mister Rabbit,
Your coat's mighty gray.
Yes, my friend,
'Twas made that way!

Mister Rabbit, Mister Rabbit,
Your feet are mighty red.
Yes, my friend,
I'm almost dead!

Mister Rabbit, Mister Rabbit,
Your tail's mighty white.
Yes, my friend,
And I'm getting
Out of sight!

TRADITIONAL

35

Six little mice sat down to spin.
Pussy passed by and she peeped in.
"What are you doing, my little men?"
"Making coats for gentlemen."
"Shall I come in and bite off your threads?"
"Oh no, Miss Pussy, you'd bite off our heads."
"Oh no, I'd not. I'd help you spin."
"That may be so, but you're not coming in."

MOTHER GOOSE

Cows

Half the time they munched the grass, and all the
time they lay
Down in the water-meadows, the lazy month of May,
A-chewing,
A-mooing,
To pass the hours away.

"Nice weather," said the brown cow.
"Ah," said the white.
"Grass is very tasty."
"Grass is all right."

Half the time they munched the grass, and all the
time they lay
Down in the water-meadows, the lazy month of May,
A-chewing,
A-mooing,
To pass the hours away.

"Rain coming," said the brown cow.
"Ah," said the white.
"Flies is very tiresome."
"Flies bite."

Half the time they munched the grass, and all the
time they lay
Down in the water-meadows, the lazy month of May,
A-chewing,
A-mooing,
To pass the hours away.

"Time to go," said the brown cow.
"Ah," said the white.
"Nice chat." "Very pleasant."
"Night." "Night."

Half the time they munched the grass, and all the
time they lay
Down in the water-meadows, the lazy month of May,
A-chewing,
A-mooing,
To pass the hours away.

JAMES REEVES

I Have a Little Cough, Sir

"I have a little cough, sir,
    In my little chest, sir,
All night long I cough, sir,
    I can never rest, sir,
And every time I cough, sir,
    It leaves a little pain, sir—
Cough, cough, cough, sir:
    There it is again, sir!"

"O Doctor Millikan,
    I shall surely die!"
"Yes, pretty Susan—
    So one day shall I."

ROBERT GRAVES

How much wood would a wood-chuck chuck
If a wood-chuck could chuck wood?
He would chuck as much wood as a wood-chuck
    would chuck,
If a wood-chuck could chuck wood.

FOLK RHYME

Conversation

Mousie, mousie,
Where is your little wee housie?

> Here is the door,
> Under the floor,
>> Said mousie, mousie.

Mousie, mousie,
May I come into your housie?

> You can't get in,
> You have to be thin,
>> Said mousie, mousie.

Mousie, mousie,
Won't you come out of your housie?

> I'm sorry to say
> I'm busy all day,
>> Said mousie, mousie.

ROSE FYLEMAN

Snail

Snail upon the wall,
Have you got at all
Anything to tell
About your shell?

Only this, my child—
When the wind is wild,
Or when the sun is hot,
It's all I've got.

JOHN DRINKWATER

Are you the guy
That told the guy
That I'm the guy
That gave the guy
The black eye?

No, I'm not the guy
That told the guy
That you're the guy
That gave the guy
The black eye!

FOLK RHYME

Little Piggy

Where are you going, you little pig?
I'm leaving my mother, I'm growing so big!
  So big, young pig!
  So young, so big!
What, leaving your mother, you foolish young pig?

Where are you going, you little pig?
I've got a new spade, and I'm going to dig!
  To dig, little pig!
  A little pig dig!
Well, I never saw a pig with a spade that could dig!

Where are you going, you little pig?
Why, I'm going to have a nice ride in a gig!
  In a gig, little pig!
  What, a pig in a gig!
Well, I never yet saw a pig in a gig!

Where are you going, you little pig?
I'm going to the barber's to buy me a wig!
  A wig, little pig!
  A pig in a wig!
Why, whoever before saw a pig in a wig!

Where are you going, you little pig?
Why, I'm going to the ball to dance a fine jig!
  A jig, little pig!
  A pig dance a jig!
Well, I never before saw a pig dance a jig!

THOMAS HOOD

Country Cat

"Where are you going, Mrs. Cat,
All by your lonesome lone?"
"Hunting a mouse, or maybe a rat
Where the ditches are overgrown."

"But you're very far from your house and home,
You've come a long, long way—"
"The further I wander, the longer I roam
The more I find mice at play."

"But you're very near to the dark pinewood
And foxes go hunting too."
"I know that a fox might find me good,
But what is a cat to do?

"I have my kittens who must be fed,
I *can't* have them skin and bone!"
And Mrs. Cat shook her brindled head
And went off by her lonesome lone.

ELIZABETH COATSWORTH

Old Shellover

"Come!" said Old Shellover.
"What?" says Creep.
"The horny old Gardener's fast asleep;
The fat cock Thrush
To his nest has gone;
And the dew shines bright
In the rising Moon;
Old Sallie Worm from her hole doth peep:
Come!" said Old Shellover.
"Ay!" said Creep.

WALTER DE LA MARE

Who Killed Cock Robin?

Who killed Cock Robin?
I, said the Sparrow,
With my bow and arrow,
I killed Cock Robin.

Who saw him die?
I, said the Fly,
With my little eye,
I saw him die.

Who caught his blood?
I, said the Fish,
With my little dish
I caught his blood.

Who'll make the shroud?
I, said the Beetle,
With my thread and needle
I'll make the shroud.

Who'll dig his grave?
I, said the Owl,
With my pick and shovel,
I'll dig his grave.

Who'll be the parson?
I, said the Rook,
With my little book,
I'll be the parson.

Who'll be the clerk?
I, said the Lark,
If it's not in the dark,
I'll be the clerk.

Who'll carry the link?
I, said the Linnet,
I'll fetch it in a minute.
I'll carry the link.

Who'll be chief mourner?
I, said the Dove,
I'll mourn for my love,
I'll be chief mourner.

Who'll carry the coffin?
I, said the Kite,
If it's not through the night,
I'll carry the coffin.

Who'll bear the pall?
We, said the Wren,
Both the cock and the hen,
We'll bear the pall.

Who'll sing a psalm?
I, said the Thrush,
As she sat on a bush,
I'll sing a psalm.

Who'll toll the bell?
I, said the Bull,
Because I can pull,
I'll toll the bell.

All the birds of the air
Fell a-sighing and a-sobbing,
When they heard the bell toll
For poor Cock Robin.

MOTHER GOOSE

WHOOO?

WHO . . . OOO?
said the owl
in the dark old tree.

WHEEEEEEEEEEEE!
said the wind
with a howl.
WHEEEEEEEEEEEE!

WHO . . . OOOOOO?
WHEEEEE . . . EEEE!

WHOOOOOO?
WHEEEEEE!

They didn't
scare
each other,
but they did
scare
WHOOO?
Me!

A dog and a cat went out together,
To see some friends just out of town;
    Said the cat to the dog,
    "What d'ye think of the weather?"
    "I think, ma'am, the rain will come down;
But don't be alarmed, for I've an umbrella
That will shelter us both," said this amiable fellow.

ANONYMOUS

The Old Man and the Bee

There was an Old Man in a tree,
Who was horribly bored by a bee;
    When they said, "Does it buzz?"
    He replied, "Yes, it does!
It's a regular brute of a bee!"

EDWARD LEAR

Who has seen the wind?
 Neither I nor you:
But when the leaves hang trembling
 The wind is passing thro'.

Who has seen the wind?
 Neither you nor I:
But when the trees bow down their heads
 The wind is passing by.

CHRISTINA ROSSETTI

O Clouds

O clouds, so white against the sky,
O seeds of milkweed drifting by,
where is the place to which you go?

"The wind has orders.
He will know."

ELIZABETH COATSWORTH

If a pig wore a wig,
    What could we say?
Treat him as gentleman,
    And say "Good day."

If his tail chanced to fail,
    What could we do?—
Send him to the tailoress
    To get one new.

CHRISTINA ROSSETTI

"To bed! To bed!"
    Says Sleepy-head.
"Tarry a while," says Slow.
    "Put on the pan,"
    Says Greedy Ann,
"Let's sup before we go."

MOTHER GOOSE

How much do you love me?
How much do you love me?
A bushel and a peck
And a hug around the neck,
That's how much I love you.

FOLK RHYME

Ladybird, Ladybird

Ladybird, Ladybird,
where do you hide?

Under a leaf on its
feathery side;
safe from the lightning—
and safe from the rain—
here I shall stay till
the sun shines again.

IVY O. EASTWICK

Pudden Tame

What's your name?
Pudden Tame.
What's your other?
Bread and Butter.
Where do you live?
In a sieve.
What's your number?
Cucumber.

FOLK RHYME

Vermont Conversation

"Good weather for hay."
"Yes, 'tis."
"Mighty bright day."
"That's true."
"Crops comin' on?"
"Yep. You?"
"Tol'rable; beans got the blight."
"Way o' the Lord."
"That's right."

PATRICIA HUBBELL

Tell Me, Tell Me, Sarah Jane

Tell me, tell me, Sarah Jane,
    Tell me, dearest daughter,
Why are you holding in your hand
    A thimbleful of water?
Why do you hold it to your eye
    And gaze both late and soon
From early morning light until
    The rising of the moon?

Mother, I hear the mermaids cry,
    I hear the mermen sing,
And I can see the sailing ships
    All made of sticks and string.
And I can see the jumping fish,
    The whales that fall and rise
And swim about the waterspout
    That swarms up to the skies.

Tell me, tell me, Sarah Jane,
    Tell your darling mother,
Why do you walk beside the tide
    As though you loved none other?
Why do you listen to a shell
    And watch the waters curl,
And throw away your diamond ring
    And wear instead the pearl?

Mother, I hear the water
Beneath the headland pinned,
And I can see the sea gull
Sliding down the wind.
I taste the salt upon my tongue
As sweet as sweet can be.

Tell me, my dear, whose voice you hear?

It is the sea, the sea.

CHARLES CAUSLEY

"Hello, Bill."
"Where are you going, Bill?"
"Downtown, Bill."
"What for, Bill?"
"To pay my gas bill."
"How much, Bill?"
"A ten dollar bill."
"So long, Bill."

FOLK RHYME

53

Imaginary Dialogues

Said Marcia Brown to Carlos Baker,
"I can't get salt from this saltshaker!"
"Just try turning it upside down!"
Said Carlos Baker to Marcia Brown.

Said Ogden Nash to Phyllis McGinley,
"I like my ham sliced rather thinly."
"I'd slice it for you, but I must dash!"
Said Phyllis McGinley to Ogden Nash.

Said Dorothy Hughes to Helen Hocking,
"I can't for the life of me get on this stocking!"
"Would it help if you first removed your shoes?"
Said Helen Hocking to Dorothy Hughes.

WILLIAM JAY SMITH

There was an old person of Ware,
Who rode on the back of a bear:
　　When they ask'd, "Does it trot?"
　　He said, "Certainly not!
He's a Moppsikon Floppsikon bear!"

EDWARD LEAR

54

Witch, Witch

"Witch, witch, where do you fly?" ...
"Under the clouds and over the sky."

"Witch, witch, what do you eat?" ...
"Little black apples from Hurricane Street."

"Witch, witch, what do you drink?" ...
"Vinegar, blacking, and good red ink."

"Witch, witch, where do you sleep?" ...
"Up in the clouds where pillows are cheap."

ROSE FYLEMAN

Mouse and Mouser

The Mouse went to visit the Cat, and found her sitting
behind the hall door, spinning.

MOUSE.
What are you doing, my lady, my lady,
What are you doing, my lady?

CAT (*sharply*).
I'm spinning old breeches, good body, good body,
I'm spinning old breeches, good body.

55

MOUSE.
Long may you wear them, my lady, my lady,
Long may you wear them, my lady.

CAT (*gruffly*).
I'll wear 'em and tear 'em, good body, good body,
I'll wear 'em and tear 'em, good body.

MOUSE.
I was sweeping my room, my lady, my lady,
I was sweeping my room, my lady.

CAT.
The cleaner you'd be, good body, good body,
The cleaner you'd be, good body.

MOUSE.
I found a silver sixpence, my lady, my lady,
I found a silver sixpence, my lady.

CAT.
The richer you were, good body, good body,
The richer you were, good body.

MOUSE.
I went to the market, my lady, my lady,
I went to the market, my lady.

CAT.
The further you went, good body, good body,
The further you went, good body.

MOUSE.
I bought me a pudding, my lady, my lady,
I bought me a pudding, my lady.

CAT (*snarling*).
The more meat you had, good body, good body,
The more meat you had, good body.

MOUSE.
I put it in the window to cool, my lady,
I put it in the window to cool.

CAT (*sharply*).
The faster you'd eat it, good body, good body,
The faster you'd eat it, good body.

MOUSE (*timidly*).
The cat came and ate it, my lady, my lady,
The cat came and ate it, my lady.

CAT (*pouncingly*).
And I'll eat you, good body, good body,
And I'll eat you, good body.

(Springs upon the mouse and kills it.)

ENGLISH FOLK TALE

Puppy and I

I met a man as I went walking;
We got talking,
Man and I.
"Where are you going to, Man?" I said
(I said to the man as he went by).
"Down to the village, to get some bread.
Will you come with me?" "No, not I."

I met a Horse as I went walking;
We got talking,
Horse and I.
"Where are you going to, Horse, today?"
(I said to the Horse as he went by).
"Down to the village to get some hay.
Will you come with me?" "No, not I."

I met a Woman as I went walking;
We got talking,
Woman and I.
"Where are you going to, Woman, so early?"
(I said to the Woman as she went by).
"Down to the village to get some barley.
Will you come with me?" "No, not I."

I met some Rabbits as I went walking;
We got talking,
Rabbits and I.

"Where are you going in your brown fur coats?"
(I said to the Rabbits as they went by).
"Down to the village to get some oats.
Will you come with us?" "No, not I."

I met a Puppy as I went walking;
We got talking,
Puppy and I.
"Where are you going this nice fine day?"
(I said to the Puppy as he went by).
"Up in the hills to roll and play."
"*I'll* come with you, Puppy," said I.

A. A. MILNE

Tadpoles

Ten little tadpoles playing in a pool,
"Come," said the water-rat, "come along to school.
Come and say your tables, sitting in a row;"
And all the little tadpoles said, "No, no, no!"

Ten little tadpoles swimming in and out,
Racing and diving and turning round about.
"Come," said their mother, "dinner-time I guess;"
And all the little tadpoles cried, "Yes, yes, yes!"

ROSE FYLEMAN

The Song of the Mad Prince

Who said, "Peacock Pie"?
  The old King to the sparrow:
Who said, "Crops are ripe"?
  Rust to the harrow:
Who said, "Where sleeps she now?
  Where rests she now her head,
Bathed in eve's loveliness"?—
  That's what I said.

Who said, "Ay, mum's the word"?
  Sexton to willow:
Who said, "Green dusk for dreams,
  Moss for a pillow"?
Who said, "All Time's delight
  Hath she for narrow bed;
Life's troubled bubble broken"?—
  That's what I said.

WALTER DE LA MARE

The Tickle Rhyme

"Who's that tickling my back?" said the wall.
"Me," said a small
Caterpillar. "I'm learning
To crawl."

IAN SERRAILLIER

Meet-on-the-Road

"Now, pray, where are you going, child?"
said Meet-on-the-Road.
"To school, sir, to school, sir,"
said Child-as-It-Stood.

"What have you in your basket, child?"
said Meet-on-the-Road.
"My dinner, sir, my dinner, sir,"
said Child-as-It-Stood.

"What have you for your dinner, child?"
said Meet-on-the-Road.
"Some pudding, sir, some pudding, sir,"
said Child-as-It-Stood.

"Oh, then I pray, give me a share,"
said Meet-on-the-Road.
"I've little enough for myself, sir,"
said Child-as-It-Stood.

"What have you got that cloak on for?"
said Meet-on-the-Road
"To keep the wind and cold from me,"
said Child-as-It-Stood

"I wish the wind would blow through you,"
said Meet-on-the-Road.
"Oh, what a wish! Oh, what a wish!"
said Child-as-It-Stood.

"Pray, what are those bells ringing for?"
said Meet-on-the-Road.
"To ring bad spirits home again,"
said Child-as-It-Stood.

"Oh, then, I must be going, child!"
said Meet-on-the-Road.
"So fare you well, so fare you well,"
said Child-as-It-Stood.

OLD ENGLISH POEM

Pirate Captain Jim

"Walk the plank," says Pirate Jim.
"But Captain Jim, I cannot swim."
"Then you must steer us through the gale."
"But Captain Jim, I cannot sail."
"Then down with the galley slaves you go."
"But Captain Jim, I cannot row."
"Then you must be the pirate's clerk."
"But Captain Jim, I cannot work."
"Then a pirate captain you must be."
"Thank you, Jim," says Captain Me.

SHEL SILVERSTEIN

Roosters

"Get out of my way!"
　　says Rooster One.
"I won't!"
　　says Rooster Two.
"You won't?"
"I won't!"
"You shall!"
"I shan't!"
Cock cock a
doodle doo!

They pecked.
They kicked.
They fought for hours.
There was a great
to-do!
"You're a very fine fighter,"
　　says Rooster One.
"You're right!"
　　says Rooster Two.

ELIZABETH COATSWORTH

Banbury Fair

"Where have you been,
    Miss Marjorie Keen?"
"To Banbury Fair,
    In a carriage and pair."
"And what could there be
    That was funny to see?"
"A dame in a wig
    A-dancing a jig."
"And what did you get
    For six pennies, my pet?"
"A pink sugar mouse
    And a gingerbread house."

EDITH G. MILLARD

Did you eever, iver, over,
In your leef, life, loaf,
See the deevel, divel, dovel,
Kiss his weef, wife, woaf?

No, I neever, niver, nover,
In my leef, life, loaf,
Saw the deevel, divel, dovel,
Kiss his weef, wife, woaf.

FOLK RHYME

Billy Boy

Billy Boy, Billy Boy, where are you riding to?
Riding Old Dobbin to Banbury Fair.
Billy Boy, Billy Boy, shall you be long away?
Just twice as long as it takes to get there.

Billy Boy, Billy Boy, what will you bring for me?
One golden fiddle to play a fine tune,
Two magic wishes and three fairy fishes,
And four rainbow ropes to climb up to the moon.

DOROTHY KING

"Who's that ringing at the front door bell?"
    Miau! Miau! Miau!
"I'm a little Pussy Cat and I'm not very well!"
    Miau! Miau! Miau!
"Then rub your nose in a bit of mutton fat."
    Miau! Miau! Miau!
"For that's the way to cure a little Pussy Cat."
    Miau! Miau! Miau!

NURSERY RHYME

"Fire! Fire!"
Cried Mrs. McGuire.
"Where! Where!"
Cried Mrs. Blair.
"All over town!"
Cried Mrs. Brown.
"Get some water!"
Cried Mrs. Carter.
"We'd better jump!"
Cried Mrs. Gump.
"That would be silly!"
Cried Mrs. Brunelli.
"It looks too risky!"
Cried Mrs. Matruski.
"What'll we do?"
Cried Mrs. LaRue.
"Turn in an alarm!"
Cried Mrs. Storm.
"Save us! Save us!"
Cried Mrs. Davis.

The fire department got
    the call
And the firemen saved
    them, one and all.

FOLK RHYME

Characterizations

Henry VIII
1509

Bluff King Hal was full of beans;
He married half a dozen queens;
For three called Kate they cried the banns,
And one called Jane, and a couple of Annes.

The first he asked to share his reign
Was Kate of Aragon, straight from Spain—
But when his love for her was spent,
He got a divorce, and out she went.

Anne Boleyn was his second wife;
He swore to cherish her all his life—
But seeing a third he wished instead,
He chopped off poor Anne Boleyn's head.

He married the next afternoon
Jane Seymour, which was rather soon—
But after one year as his bride
She crept into her bed and died.

Anne of Cleves was Number Four;
Her portrait thrilled him to the core—
But when he met her face to face
Another royal divorce took place.

Catherine Howard, Number Five,
Billed and cooed to keep alive—

But one day Henry felt depressed;
The executioner did the rest.

Sixth and last came Catherine Parr,
Sixth and last and luckiest far—
For this time it was Henry who
Hopped the twig, and a good job too.

ELEANOR AND HERBERT FARJEON

John
1199

John, John, bad King John,
Shamed the throne that he sat on;
Not a scruple, not a straw,
Cared this monarch for the law;
Promises he daily broke;
None could trust a word he spoke;
So the Barons brought a Deed
Down to rushy Runnymede,
Magna Carta was it hight,
Charter of the People's Right,
Framed and fashioned to correct
Kings who act with disrespect—
And with stern and solemn air,
Pointing to the parchment there,
"Sign! sign! sign!" they said,
"Sign, King John, or resign instead!"

John, John, turning pale,
Ground his teeth, and bit his nail;
Chewed his long moustache; and then
Ground and bit and chewed again.
"Plague upon the People!" he
Muttered, "what are they to me?
Plague upon the Barons, too!"
(Here he had another chew.)
But the Barons, standing by,
Eyed him with a baleful eye;
Not a finger did they lift;
Not an eyelash did they shift;
But with one tremendous roar,
Even louder than before,
" *Sign! sign! sign!*" they said,
"SIGN, KING JOHN, OR RESIGN INSTEAD!"

[And King John signed.]

ELEANOR AND HERBERT FARJEON

Tom tied a kettle to the tail of a cat,
Jill put a stone in the blind man's hat,
Bob threw his grandmother down the stairs—
And they all grew up ugly, and nobody cares.

FOLK RHYME

Richard III
1483

Crookback Dick
  Had nephews two,
Younger than me,
  Older than you.

Crookback Dick,
  He spoke them fair,
One was king,
  The other was heir.

Crookback Dick,
  He longed for power,
So he smothered his nephews
  In the Tower.

Nobody dared
  To say a word,
And Crookback Dick
  Became Richard the Third.

ELEANOR AND HERBERT FARJEON

Peregrine White and Virginia Dare
1620　　　　1587

Peregrine White
And Virginia Dare
Were the first real Americans
Anywhere.

Others might find it
Strange to come
Over the ocean
To make a home.

England and memory
Left behind—
But Virginia and Peregrine
Didn't mind.

One of them born
On Roanoke,
And the other cradled
In Pilgrim oak.

Rogues might bicker
And good men pray.
Did they pay attention?
No, not they.

Men might grumble
And women weep

But Virginia and Peregrine
Went to sleep.

They had their dinner
And napped and then
When they woke up
It was dinner again.

They didn't worry,
They didn't wish,
They didn't farm
And they didn't fish.

There was lots of work
But they didn't do it.
They were pioneers
But they never knew it.

Wolves in the forest
And Indian drums!
Virginia and Peregrine
Sucked their thumbs.

They were only babies.
They didn't care.
Peregrine White
And Virginia Dare.

ROSEMARY AND STEPHEN VINCENT BENÉT

The Microscope

Anton Leeuwenhoek was Dutch.
He sold pincushions, cloth, and such.
The waiting townsfolk fumed and fussed
As Anton's dry goods gathered dust.

He worked, instead of tending store,
At grinding special lenses for
A microscope. Some of the things
He looked at were:
                    mosquitoes' wings,
the hairs of sheep, the legs of lice,
the skin of people, dogs, and mice;
ox eyes, spiders' spinning gear,
fishes' scales, a little smear
of his own blood,
                    and best of all,
the unknown, busy, very small
bugs that swim and bump and hop
inside a simple water drop.

Impossible! Most Dutchmen said.
This Anton's crazy in the head.
We ought to ship him off to Spain.
He says he's seen a housefly's brain.
He says the water that we drink
Is full of bugs. He's mad, we think!
They called him *dumkopf*, which means dope.
That's how we got the microscope.

MAXINE KUMIN

Song

"I like birds," said the Dryad,
"and the murmuring of trees,
and stars seen through dark branches,
and mumbling, bumbling bees,
I like the forest and its smells and its shadows,
I like all of these."

"I like fish," said the Mermaid,
"and the sharp rustle of waves,
and the branching shapes of corals
that grow on seamen's graves,
I like the wetness and the depth and the silence,
I like green caves."

ELIZABETH COATSWORTH

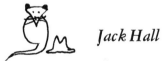 *Jack Hall*

Jack Hall
He is so small,
A mouse could eat him,
Hat and all.

NURSERY RHYME

75

Mrs. Utter

Poor Mrs. Utter,
She eats no butter
But gristly meat and horrible pies,
With a mug of sour ale
And a loaf that is stale
And a withered brown fish with buttony eyes!

In a black tattered skirt
She kneels in the dirt
And clatters her dustpan and brush on the stairs;
But everything's dusty
And musty and rusty,
For the pump-handle's broken, the broom has no hairs.

The roof-top is leaky,
The window-frames squeaky,
And out of the chimney the fledgelings fly.
Beside the bare grate
Lies old scraggy Kate,
A cat with one ear and one emerald eye.

Poor Mrs. Utter
Would mumble and mutter,
"Ah! this is no life for a Princess of Spain.
I once had fine fare
And silk clothes to wear,
Ah me, shall I ever be rich again?"

JAMES REEVES

The Purist

I give you now Professor Twist,
A conscientious scientist.
Trustees exclaimed, "He never bungles!"
And sent him off to distant jungles.
Camped on a tropic riverside,
One day he missed his loving bride.
She had, the guide informed him later,
Been eaten by an alligator.
Professor Twist could not but smile.
"You mean," he said, "a crocodile."

OGDEN NASH

Amelia Mixed the Mustard

Amelia mixed the mustard,
    She mixed it good and thick;
She put it in the custard
    And made her Mother sick,
And showing satisfaction
    By many a loud huzza
"Observe" said she "the action
    Of mustard on Mamma."

A. E. HOUSMAN

Daniel

Darius the Mede was a king and a wonder.
His eye was proud, and his voice was thunder.
He kept bad lions in a monstrous den.
He fed up the lions on Christian men.

Daniel was the chief hired man of the land.
He stirred up the music in the palace band.
He whitewashed the cellar. He shovelled in the coal.
And Daniel kept a-praying:—"Lord save my soul."
Daniel kept a-praying:—"Lord save my soul."
Daniel kept a-praying:—"Lord save my soul."

Daniel was the butler, swagger and swell.
He ran upstairs. He answered the bell.
And *he* would let in whoever came a-calling:—
Saints so holy, scamps so appalling.
"Old man Ahab leaves his card.
Elisha and bears are a-waiting in the yard.
Here comes Pharaoh and his snakes a-calling.
Here comes Cain and his wife a-calling.
Shadrach, Meshach and Abednego for tea.
Here comes Jonah and the whale,
And the *Sea*!
Here comes St. Peter and his fishing pole.
Here comes Judas and his silver a-calling.
Here comes old Beelzebub a-calling."
And Daniel kept a-praying:—"Lord save my soul."

Daniel kept a-praying:—"Lord save my soul."
Daniel kept a-praying:—"Lord save my soul."

His sweetheart and his mother were Christian and meek.
They washed and ironed for Darius every week.
One Thursday he met them at the door:—
Paid them as usual, but acted sore.

He said:—"Your Daniel is a dead little pigeon.
He's a good hard worker, but he talks religion."
And he showed them Daniel in the lions' cage.
Daniel standing quietly, the lions in a rage.
His good old mother cried:—
"Lord save him."
And Daniel's tender sweetheart cried:—
"Lord save him."

And she was a golden lily in the dew.
And she was as sweet as an apple on the tree,
And she was as fine as a melon in the corn-field,
Gliding and lovely as a ship on the sea,
Gliding and lovely as a ship on the sea.

And she prayed to the Lord:—
"*Send* Gabriel. *Send* Gabriel."

King Darius said to the lions:—
"Bite Daniel. Bite Daniel.
Bite him. Bite him. Bite him!"

Thus roared the lions:—

79

"We want Daniel, Daniel, Daniel,
We want Daniel, Daniel, Daniel."
Grrrrrrrrrrrrrrrrrrrrrrrrrrrrrrrrrrrrrrrrrr
Grrrrrrrrrrrrrrrrrrrrrrrrrrrrrrrrrrrrrrrrrr

And Daniel did not frown,
Daniel did not cry.
He kept looking at the sky.
And the Lord said to Gabriel:—
"Go chain the lions down,
Go chain the lions down.
Go chain the lions down.
Go chain the lions down."

And *Gabriel* chained the lions,
And *Gabriel* chained the lions,
And *Gabriel* chained the lions,
And Daniel got out of the den,
And Daniel got out of the den,
And Daniel got out of the den.
And Darius said:—"You're a Christian child,"
Darius said:—"You're a Christian child,"
Darius said:—"You're a Christian child,"
And gave him his job again,
And gave him his job again,
And gave him his job again.

VACHEL LINDSAY

80

The Young Lady of Lynn

There was a young lady of Lynn
Who was so excessively thin
    That when she essayed
    To drink lemonade
She slipped through the straw and fell in.

ANONYMOUS

Chang McTang McQuarter Cat

Chang McTang McQuarter Cat
Is one part this and one part that.
One part is yowl, one part is purr.
One part is scratch, one part is fur.
One part, maybe even two,
Is how he sits and stares right through
You and you and you and you.
And when you feel my Chang-Cat stare
You wonder if you're really there.

Chang McTang McQuarter Cat
Is one part this and ten parts that.
He's one part saint, and two parts sin.
One part yawn, and three parts grin,
One part sleepy, four parts lightning,
One part cuddly, five parts fright'ning,
One part snarl, and six parts play.
One part is how he goes away
Inside himself, somewhere miles back
Behind his eyes, somewhere as black
And green and yellow as the night
A jungle makes in full moonlight.

Chang McTang McQuarter Cat
Is one part this and twenty that.
One part is statue, one part tricks—
(One part, or six, or thirty-six.)

One part (or twelve, or sixty-three)
Is—Chang McTang belongs to ME!

Don't ask, "How many parts is that?"
Addition's nothing to a cat.

If you knew Chang, then you'd know this:
He's one part everything there is.

JOHN CIARDI

Mrs. Golightly

Mrs. Golightly's goloshes
  Are roomy and large;
Through water she slithers and sloshes,
  As safe as a barge.

When others at home must be stopping,
  To market she goes,
And returns later on with her shopping
  Tucked into her toes.

JAMES REEVES

Eat-It-All Elaine

I went away last August
To summer camp in Maine,
And there I met a camper
Called Eat-it-all Elaine.
Although Elaine was quiet,
She liked to cause a stir
By acting out the nickname
Her camp-mates gave to her.

The day of our arrival
At Cabin Number Three
When girls kept coming over
To greet Elaine and me,
She took a piece of Kleenex
And calmly chewed it up,
Then strolled outside the cabin
And ate a buttercup.

Elaine, from that day forward,
Was always in command.
On hikes, she'd eat some birch-bark
On swims, she'd eat some sand.
At meals, she'd swallow prune-pits
And never have a pain,
While everyone around her
Would giggle, "Oh, Elaine!"

One morning, berry-picking,
A bug was in her pail,
And though we thought for certain
Her appetite would fail,
Elaine said, "Hmm, a stinkbug."
And while we murmured, "Ooh,"
She ate her pail of berries
And ate the stinkbug, too.

The night of Final Banquet
When counselors were handing
Awards to different children
Whom they believed outstanding,
To every *thinking* person
At summer camp in Maine
The Most Outstanding Camper
Was Eat-it-all Elaine.

KAYE STARBIRD

I Want You to Meet ...

... Meet Ladybug,
her little sister Sadiebug,
her mother, Mrs. Gradybug,
her aunt, that nice oldmaidybug,
and Baby—she's a fraidybug.

DAVID MCCORD

Miss T.

It's a very odd thing—
   As odd as can be—
That whatever Miss T. eats
   Turns into Miss T.;
Porridge and apples,
   Mince, muffins and mutton,
Jam, junket, jumbles—
   Not a rap, not a button
It matters; the moment
   They're out of her plate,
Though shared by Miss Butcher
   And sour Mr. Bate,
Tiny and cheerful,
   And neat as can be,
Whatever Miss T. eats
   Turns into Miss T.

WALTER DE LA MARE

Around and around a dusty little room,
Went a very little maiden with a very big broom.
And she said, "Oh, I could make it so tidy and so trig,
Were I a little bigger and my broom not quite so big!"

MARGARET JOHNSON

86

Mrs. Malone

Mrs. Malone
Lived hard by a wood
All on her lonesome
As nobody should.
With her crust on a plate
And her pot on the coal
And none but herself
To converse with, poor soul.
In a shawl and a hood
She got sticks out-o'-door,
On a bit of old sacking
She slept on the floor,
And nobody, nobody
Asked how she fared
Or knew how she managed,
For nobody cared.
    Why make a pother
    About an old crone?
    What for should they bother
    With Mrs. Malone?

One Monday in winter
With snow on the ground
So thick that a footstep
Fell without sound,
She heard a faint frostbitten

Peck on the pane
And went to the window
To listen again.
There sat a cock-sparrow
Bedraggled and weak,
With half-open eyelid
And ice on his beak.
She threw up the sash
And she took the bird in,
And mumbled and fumbled it
Under her chin.
　　"Ye're all of a smother,
　　Ye're fair overblown!
　　I've room fer another,"
　　Said Mrs. Malone.

Come Tuesday while eating
Her dry morning slice
With the sparrow a-picking
("Ain't company nice!")
She heard on her doorpost
A curious scratch,
And there was a cat
With its claw on the latch.
It was hungry and thirsty
And thin as a lath,
It mewed and it mowed
On the slithery path.

She threw the door open
And warmed up some pap,
And huddled and cuddled it
In her old lap.
    "There, there, little brother,
    Ye poor skin-an'-bone,
    There's room fer another,"
    Said Mrs. Malone.

Come Wednesday while all of them
Crouched on the mat
With a crumb for the sparrow,
A sip for the cat,
There was wailing and whining
Outside in the wood,
And there sat a vixen
With six of her brood.
She was haggard and ragged
And worn to a shred,
And her half-dozen babies
Were only half-fed,
But Mrs. Malone, crying
"My! ain't they sweet!"
Happed them and lapped them
And gave them to eat.
    "You warm yerself, mother,
    Ye're cold as a stone!
    There's room fer another,"
    Said Mrs. Malone.

Come Thursday a donkey
Stepped in off the road
With sores on his withers
From bearing a load.
Come Friday when icicles
Pierced the white air
Down from the mountainside
Lumbered a bear.
For each she had something,
If little, to give—
"Lord knows, the poor critters
Must all of 'em live."
She gave them her sacking,
Her hood and her shawl,
Her loaf and her teapot—
She gave them her all.
    "What with one thing and t'other
    Me fambily's grown,
    And there's room fer another,"
    Said Mrs. Malone.

Come Saturday evening
When time was to sup
Mrs. Malone
Had forgot to sit up.
The cat said *meeow*,
And the sparrow said *peep*,
The vixen, *she's sleeping*,
The bear, *let her sleep*.

On the back of the donkey
They bore her away,
Through trees and up mountains
Beyond night and day,
Till come Sunday morning
They brought her in state
Through the last cloudbank
As far as the Gate.
        "Who is it," asked Peter,
        "You have with you there?"
        And donkey and sparrow,
        Cat, vixen and bear

Exclaimed, "Do you tell us
Up here she's unknown?
It's our mother, God bless us!
It's Mrs. Malone
Whose havings were few
And whose holding was small
And whose heart was so big
It had room for us all."
Then Mrs. Malone
Of a sudden awoke,
She rubbed her two eyeballs
And anxiously spoke:
"Where am I, to goodness,
And what do I see?
My dears, let's turn back,
This ain't no place fer me!"

But Peter said, "Mother
Go in to the Throne.
There's room for another
One, Mrs. Malone."

ELEANOR FARJEON

Almost

Peterboo and Prescott
And pretty Pam, too,
Are very many children
But they know what to do,

They eat all their cereal
And crusts of their bread,
They never need spankings,
They go quietly to bed,

They hang up their clothes,
They practice when they should,
And their manners are always
Exceptionally good.

This little poem
Is about Peterboo
And Pamela and Prescott—
And it's *almost* true.

HARRY BEHN

Mrs. Button

When Mrs. Button, of a morning,
　　Comes creaking down the street,
You hear her old two black boots whisper
　　"Poor feet—poor feet—poor feet!"

When Mrs. Button, every Monday,
　　Sweeps the chapel neat,
All down the long, hushed aisles they whisper
　　"Poor feet—poor feet—poor feet!"

Mrs. Button after dinner
　　(It is her Sunday treat)
Sits down and takes her two black boots off
　　And rests her two poor feet.

JAMES REEVES

Peculiar

I once knew a boy who was odd as could be:
He liked to eat cauliflower and broccoli
And spinach and turnips and rhubarb pies
And he didn't like hamburgers or French fries.

EVE MERRIAM

The Witch's Garden

In the witch's
garden
the gate is open
wide.

"Come inside,"
says the
witch.
"Dears,
come inside.

No flowers
in MY garden
nothing mint-y
nothing chive-y.

Come inside,
come inside.
See my lovely
poison ivy."

LILIAN MOORE

Clock

This clock
Has stopped,
Some gear
Or spring
Gone wrong—
Too tight,
Or cracked,
Or choked
With dust;
A year
Has passed
Since last
It said
Ting ting
Or tick
Or tock.
Poor
Clock.

VALERIE WORTH

Cow

The cow
Coming
Across the grass
Moves
Like a mountain
Toward us;
Her hipbones
Jut
Like sharp
Peaks
Of stone,
Her hoofs
Thump
Like dropped
Rocks:
Almost
Too late
She stops.

VALERIE WORTH

Whale

A whale is stout about the middle,
He is stout about the ends,
& so is all his family
& so are all his friends.

He's pleased that he's enormous,
He's happy he weighs tons,
& so are all his daughters
& so are all his sons.

He eats when he is hungry
Each kind of food he wants,
& so do all his uncles
& so do all his aunts.

He doesn't mind his blubber,
He doesn't mind his creases,
& neither do his nephews
& neither do his nieces.

You may find him chubby,
You may find him fat,
But he would disagree with you:
He likes himself like that.

MARY ANN HOBERMAN

My Grasshopper

My grasshopper died
near the daisy bed,
fell on his back,
bumped his head
and kicked his feet into the air,
and someone swept him off somewhere.

MYRA COHN LIVINGSTON

Doors

An open door says, "Come in."
A shut door says, "Who are you?"
Shadows and ghosts go through shut doors.
If a door is shut and you want it shut,
    why open it?
If a door is open and you want it open,
    why shut it?
Doors forget but only doors know what it is
    doors forget.

CARL SANDBURG

Fish

Fish have fins
and fish have tails;
fish have skins
concealed by scales.
Fish are seldom
found on land;
fish would rather
swim than stand.

JACK PRELUTSKY

Bees

Every bee
that
ever was
was
partly
sting
and partly
. . . buzz.

JACK PRELUTSKY

The Dodo

Oh when the dodo flourished
What did the dodo do?
The dodo had such stubby wings
The dodo never flew.

Oh when the dodo had his day
What was the dodo's plan?
The dodo had such stumpy legs
The dodo never ran.

The prey of human predators,
A bird who couldn't soar,
With all his brood pursued for food
The dodo is no more.

And now, alas, the dodo's read as
Simply something to be dead as.

ISABEL WILNER

The Prudent Rodent

The prudent rodent wouldn't bite
Upon the bait set out at night,
And because the rodent wouldn't
The trap that might have caught him couldn't.

ISABEL WILNER

True

When
the green eyes
of a cat
look deep into
you

you know
that
whatever it is
they are saying
is
true.

LILIAN MOORE

103

Worms and the Wind

Worms would rather be worms.
Ask a worm and he says, "Who knows what a worm
knows?"
Worms go down and up and over and under.
Worms like tunnels.
When worms talk they talk about the worm world.
Worms like it in the dark.
Neither the sun nor the moon interests a worm.
Zigzag worms hate circle worms.
Curve worms never trust square worms.
Worms know what worms want.
Slide worms are suspicious of crawl worms.
One worm asks another, "How does your belly drag
today?"
The shape of a crooked worm satisfies a crooked
worm.
A straight worm says, "Why not be straight?"
Worms tired of crawling begin to slither.
Long worms slither farther than short worms.
Middle-sized worms say, "It is nice to be neither long
nor short."
Old worms teach young worms to say, "Don't be
sorry for me unless you
have been a worm and lived in worm places and
read worm books."

When worms go to war they dig in, come out and
                              fight, dig in again,
      come out and fight again, dig in again, and so on.
Worms underground never hear the wind overground
                              and sometimes they
      ask, "What is this wind we hear of?"

CARL SANDBURG

Oysters

Oysters
are creatures
without
any features.

JACK PRELUTSKY

House Moving

Look! A house is being moved!
  Hoist!
  Jack!
  Line!
  Truck!

  Shout!
  Yell!
  Stop!
  Stuck!

  Cable!
  Kick!
  Jerk!
  Bump!

  Lift!
  Slide!
  Crash!
  Dump!
This crew could learn simplicity from turtles.

PATRICIA HUBBELL

106

Paper I

Paper is two kinds, to write on, to wrap with.
If you like to write, you write.
If you like to wrap, you wrap.
Some papers like writers, some like wrappers.
Are you a writer or a wrapper?

CARL SANDBURG

Paper II

I write what I know on one side of the paper
    and what I don't know on the other.
Fire likes dry paper and wet paper laughs at fire.
Empty paper sacks say, "Put something in me,
    what are we waiting for?"
Paper sacks packed to the limit say, "We hope
    we don't bust."
Paper people like to meet other paper people.

CARL SANDBURG

When the donkey saw the zebra
He began to switch his tail;
"Well I never!" said the donkey,
"There's a mule that's been to jail."

FOLK RHYME

Giraffes

I like them.
Ask me why.
    Because they hold their heads so high.
    Because their necks stretch to the sky.
    Because they're quiet, calm, and shy.
    Because they run so fast they fly.
    Because their eyes are velvet brown.
    Because their coats are spotted tan.
    Because they eat the tops of trees.
    Because their legs have knobby knees.
    Because
    Because
    Because. That's why
I like giraffes.

MARY ANN HOBERMAN

I Left My Head

I left my head
somewhere
today.
Put it down for
just
a minute.
Under the
table?
On a chair?
Wish I were
able
to say
where.
Everything I need
is
in it!

LILIAN MOORE

Hey, Bug!

Hey, bug, stay!
Don't run away.
I know a game that we can play.

I'll hold my fingers very still
and you can climb a finger-hill.

No, no.
Don't go.

Here's a wall— a tower, too,
a tiny bug town, just for you.
I've a cookie. You have some.
Take this oatmeal cookie crumb.

Hey, bug, stay!
Hey, bug!
Hey!

LILIAN MOORE

The horses of the sea
   Rear a foaming crest,
But the horses of the land
   Serve us the best.

The horses of the land
   Munch corn and clover,
While the foaming sea-horses
   Toss and turn over.

CHRISTINA ROSSETTI

Sea-Wash

The sea-wash never ends.
The sea-wash repeats, repeats.
Only old songs? Is that all the sea knows?
   Only the old strong songs?
   Is that all?
The sea-wash repeats, repeats.

CARL SANDBURG

I Think So: Don't You?

If many men knew
What many men know,
If many men went
Where many men go,
If many men did
What many men do,
The world would be better—
I think so; don't you?

If muffins and crumpets
Grew all ready toasted,
And sucking pigs ran about
All ready roasted,
And the bushes were covered
With jackets all new,
It would be convenient—
I think so; don't you?

ANONYMOUS

Red

All day
across the way
on someone's sill
a geranium glows
red bright
like a
tiny
faraway
traffic light.

LILIAN MOORE

Jill Withers Had a Farthingale

Jill Withers had a farthingale
It hid her tummy and her tail
That's why she wore her farthingale.

JOHN BECKER

The Shrew

The pygmy shrew is very small,
he almost isn't there at all.
He measures a trifle over an inch
(hardly enough for a healthy pinch).

JACK PRELUTSKY

Me

"My nose is blue,
My teeth are green,
My face is like a soup tureen.
I look just like a lima bean.
I'm very, very lovely.
My feet are far too short
And long.
My hands are left and right
And wrong.
My voice is like the hippo's song.
I'm very, very,
Very, very,
Very, very
Lovely?"

KARLA KUSKIN

Money

Workers earn it,
Spendthrifts burn it,
Bankers lend it,
Women spend it,
Forgers fake it,
Taxes take it,
Dying leave it,
Heirs receive it,
Thrifty save it,
Misers crave it,
Robbers seize it,
Rich increase it,
Gamblers lose it . . .
I could use it.

RICHARD ARMOUR

Morning

Everyone is tight asleep,
I think I'll sing a tune,
And if I sing it loud enough
I'll wake up someone—soon!

MYRA COHN LIVINGSTON

Coins

Coins are pleasant
To the hand:

Neat circles, smooth,
A little heavy.

They feel as if
They are worth something.

VALERIE WORTH

Whispers

Whispers
   tickle through your ear
   telling things you like to hear.

Whispers
   are as soft as skin
   letting little words curl in.

Whispers
   come so they can blow
   secrets others never know.

MYRA COHN LIVINGSTON

116

Stars

The stars are too many to count.
The stars make sixes and sevens.
The stars tell nothing—and everything.
The stars looked scattered.
Stars are so far away they never speak
    when spoken to.

CARL SANDBURG

This Is My Rock

This is my rock,
And here I run
To steal the secret of the sun;

This is my rock,
And here come I
Before the night has swept the sky;

This is my rock,
This is the place
I meet the evening face to face.

DAVID MCCORD

117

Sun

The sun
Is a leaping fire
Too hot
To go near,

But it will still
Lie down
In warm yellow squares
On the floor

Like a flat
Quilt, where
The cat can curl
And purr.

VALERIE WORTH

Cocoon

The little caterpillar creeps
Awhile before in silk it sleeps.
It sleeps awhile before it flies,
And flies awhile before it dies,
And that's the end of three good tries.

DAVID MCCORD

Narrations

The Three Foxes

Once upon a time there were three little foxes
Who didn't wear stockings, and they didn't wear sockses,
But they all had handkerchiefs to blow their noses,
And they kept their handkerchiefs in cardboard boxes.

They lived in the forest in three little houses,
And they didn't wear coats, and they didn't wear trousies.
They ran through the woods on their little bare tootsies,
And they played "Touch last" with a family of mouses.

They didn't go shopping in the High Street shopses,
But caught what they wanted in the woods and copses.
They all went fishing, and they caught three wormses,
They went out hunting, and they caught three wopses.

They went to a Fair, and they all won prizes—
Three plum-puddingses and three mince-pieses.
They rode on elephants and swang on swingses,
And hit three coco-nuts at coco-nut shieses.

That's all that I know of the three little foxes
Who kept their handkerchiefs in cardboard boxes.
They lived in the forest in three little houses,
But they didn't wear coats and they didn't wear trousies,
And they didn't wear stockings and they didn't wear
    sockses.

A. A. MILNE

The Walrus and the Carpenter

The sun was shining on the sea,
    Shining with all his might:
He did his very best to make
    The billows smooth and bright—
And this was odd, because it was
    The middle of the night.

The moon was shining sulkily,
    Because she thought the sun
Had got no business to be there
    After the day was done——
"It's very rude of him," she said,
    "To come and spoil the fun!"

The sea was wet as wet could be,
    The sands were dry as dry.
You could not see a cloud, because
    No cloud was in the sky:
No birds were flying overhead—
    There were no birds to fly.

The Walrus and the Carpenter
    Were walking close at hand;
They wept like anything to see
    Such quantities of sand:
"If this were only cleared away,"
    They said, "it *would* be grand!"

"If seven maids with seven mops
    Swept it for half a year,
Do you suppose," the Walrus said,
    "That they could get it clear?"
"I doubt it," said the Carpenter,
    And shed a bitter tear.

"O Oysters, come and walk with us!"
    The Walrus did beseech.
"A pleasant walk, a pleasant talk,
    Along the briny beach:
We cannot do with more than four,
    To give a hand to each."

The eldest Oyster looked at him
    But never a word he said:
The eldest Oyster winked his eye,
    And shook his heavy head—
Meaning to say he did not choose
    To leave the oyster-bed.

But four young Oysters hurried up,
    All eager for the treat:
Their coats were brushed, their faces
    washed,
    Their shoes were clean and neat—
And this was odd, because, you know,
    They hadn't any feet.

Four other Oysters followed them,
    And yet another four:

And thick and fast they came at last,
    And more, and more, and more—
All hopping through the frothy waves,
    And scrambling to the shore.

The Walrus and the Carpenter
    Walked on a mile or so,
And then they rested on a rock
    Conveniently low:
And all the little Oysters stood
    And waited in a row.

"The time has come," the Walrus said,
    "To talk of many things:
Of shoes—and ships—and sealing-wax—
    Of cabbages—and kings—
And why the sea is boiling hot—
    And whether pigs have wings."

"But wait a bit," the Oysters cried,
    "Before we have our chat;
For some of us are out of breath,
    And all of us are fat!"
"No hurry!" said the Carpenter.
    They thanked him much for that.

"A loaf of bread," the Walrus said,
    "Is what we chiefly need:
Pepper and vinegar besides
    Are very good indeed—

Now, if you're ready, Oysters dear,
    We can begin to feed."

"But not on us!" the Oysters cried,
    Turning a little blue.
"After such kindness, that would be
    A dismal thing to do!"
"The night is fine," the Walrus said.
    "Do you admire the view?

"It was so kind of you to come!
    And you are very nice!"
The Carpenter said nothing but
    "Cut us another slice.
I wish you were not quite so deaf—
    I've had to ask you twice!"

"It seems a shame," the Walrus said,
    "To play them such a trick,
After we've brought them out so far,
    And made them trot so quick!"
The Carpenter said nothing but
    "The butter's spread too thick!"

"I weep for you," the Walrus said:
    "I deeply sympathize."
With sobs and tears he sorted out
    Those of the largest size,
Holding his pocket-handkerchief
    Before his streaming eyes.

"O Oysters," said the Carpenter,
    "You've had a pleasant run!
Shall we be trotting home again?"
    But answer came there none—
And this was scarcely odd, because
    They'd eaten every one.

LEWIS CARROLL

There Once Was a Puffin

Oh, there once was a Puffin
Just the shape of a muffin,
And he lived on an island
In the
        bright
            blue
                sea!
He ate little fishes,
That were most delicious,
And he had them for supper
And he
        had
            them
                for tea.

But this poor little Puffin,
He couldn't play nothin',
For he hadn't anybody
To
    play
        with
            at all.
So he sat on his island,
And he cried for a while, and
He felt very lonely,
And he
    felt
        very small.
Then along came the fishes,
And they said, "If you wishes,
You can have us for playmates,
Instead
    of
        for
            tea!"
So they now play together,
In all sorts of weather,
And the Puffin eats pancakes,
Like you
    and
        like
            me.

FLORENCE PAGE JAQUES

Alligator on the Escalator

Through the revolving door
Of a department store
There slithered an alligator.

When he came to the escalator,
He stepped upon the track with great dexterity;
His tail draped over the railing,
And he clicked his teeth in glee:

"Yo, I'm off on the escalator,
Excited as I can be!
It's a *moving* experience,
As you can plainly see.
On the moving stair I go anywhere,
I rise to the top
Past outerwear, innerwear,
Dinnerwear, thinnerwear—
Then down to the basement with bargains galore,
Then back on the track to the top once more!
Oh, I may ride the escalator
Until closing time or later,
So tell the telephone operator
To call Mrs. Albert Q. Alligator
And tell her to take a hot mud bath
And not to wait up for me!"

EVE MERRIAM

The Owl and the Pussy-Cat

The Owl and the Pussy-Cat went to sea
    In a beautiful pea-green boat,
They took some honey, and plenty of money,
    Wrapped up in a five-pound note.
The Owl looked up to the stars above,
    And sang to a small guitar,
"O lovely Pussy! O Pussy, my love,
    "What a beautiful Pussy you are,
        "You are,
        "You are!
    "What a beautiful Pussy you are!"
Pussy said to the Owl, "You elegant fowl!
    "How charmingly sweet you sing!
"O let us be married! too long have we tarried:
    "But what shall we do for a ring?"
They sailed away for a year and a day,
    To the land where the Bong-tree grows,
And there in a wood a Piggy-wig stood,
    With a ring at the end of his nose,
        His nose,
        His nose,
    With a ring at the end of his nose.

"Dear Pig, are you willing to sell for one shilling
    "Your ring?" Said the Piggy, "I will."

So they took it away, and were married next day
    By the Turkey who lives on the hill.
They dined on mince, and slices of quince,
    Which they ate with a runcible spoon;
And hand in hand, on the edge of the sand,
    They danced by the light of the moon,
        The moon,
        The moon,
    They danced by the light of the moon.

EDWARD LEAR

The Monkeys and the Crocodile

Five little monkeys
    Swinging from a tree;
Teasing Uncle Crocodile,
    Merry as can be.
Swinging high, swinging low,
    Swinging left and right:
"Dear Uncle Crocodile,
    Come and take a bite!"

129

Five little monkeys
    Swinging in the air;
Heads up, tails up,
    Little do they care.
Swinging up, swinging down,
    Swinging far and near:
"Poor Uncle Crocodile,
    Aren't you hungry, dear?"

Four little monkeys
    Sitting in the tree;
Heads down, tails down,
    Dreary as can be.
Weeping loud, weeping low,
    Crying to each other:
"Wicked Uncle Crocodile,
    To gobble up our brother!"

LAURA E. RICHARDS

Belly & Tubs went out in a boat,
Tubs wore knickers & Belly a coat,
They got in a quarrel & started to shout
And the boat tipped over & they tumbled out.

CLYDE WATSON

130

I had a little hen,
The prettiest ever seen;
She washed up the dishes,
And kept the house clean.
She went to the mill
To fetch me some flour,
And always got home
In less than an hour.
She baked me my bread,
She brewed me my ale,
She sat by the fire
And told a fine tale.

MOTHER GOOSE

Three little Guinea pigs
went to see the King.
One brought a rose;
one brought a ring;
one brought a turnip
to give to the King.

Two went back home
neither fatter
nor thinner.
One sat on the Queen's lap
and ate the King's dinner.

N. M. BODECKER

The Grasshopper

Down
a
deep
well
a
grasshopper
fell.

By kicking about
He thought to get out.
      He might have known better,
      For that got him wetter.
To kick round and round
Is the way to get drowned,
      And drowning is what
      I should tell you he got.

But
the
well
had
a
rope
that
dangled
some
hope.

And sure as molasses
On one of his passes
      He found the rope handy
      And up he went, *and he*

it
up
and
it
up
and
it
up
and
it
up
went

And hopped away proper
As any grasshopper.

DAVID MCCORD

Way down South where bananas grow
A grasshopper stepped on an elephant's toe.
The elephant said, with tears in his eyes,
"Pick on somebody your own size."

FOLK RHYME

The Floor and the Ceiling

Winter and summer, whatever the weather,
The Floor and the Ceiling were happy together
In a quaint little house on the outskirts of town
With the Floor looking up and the Ceiling looking down.

The Floor bought the Ceiling an ostrich-plumed hat,
And they dined upon drippings of bacon fat,
Diced artichoke hearts and cottage cheese
And hundreds of other such delicacies.

On a screened-in porch in early spring
They would sit at the player piano and sing.
When the Floor cried in French, *"Ah, je vous adore!"*
The Ceiling replied, "You adorable Floor!"

The years went by as the years they will,
And each little thing was fine until
One evening, enjoying their bacon fat,
The Floor and the Ceiling had a terrible spat.

The Ceiling, loftily looking down,
Said, "You are the *lowest* Floor in this town!"
The Floor, looking up with a frightening grin,
Said, "Keep up your chatter, and *you* will cave in!"

So they went off to bed: while the Floor settled down,
The Ceiling packed up her gay wallflower gown;
And tiptoeing out past the Chippendale chair
And the gateleg table, down the stair,

Took a coat from the hook and a hat from the rack,
And flew out the door—farewell to the Floor!—
And flew out the door, and was seen no more,
And flew out the door, and *never* came back!

In a quaint little house on the outskirts of town,
Now the shutters go bang, and the walls tumble down;
And the roses in summer run wild through the room,
But blooming for no one—then why should they bloom?

For what is a Floor now that brambles have grown
Over window and woodwork and chimney of stone?
For what is a Floor when the Floor stands alone?
And what is a Ceiling when the Ceiling has flown?

WILLIAM JAY SMITH

I had a little pig,
I fed him in a trough,
He got so fat
His tail dropped off.
So I got me a hammer,
And I got me a nail,
And I made my little pig
A brand new tail.

FOLK RHYME

Knitted Things

There was a witch who knitted things:
Elephants and playground swings.
She knitted rain,
She knitted night,
But nothing really came out right.
The elephants had just one tusk
And night looked more
Like dawn or dusk.

The rain was snow
And when she tried
To knit an egg
It came out fried.
She knitted birds
With buttonholes
And twenty rubber butter rolls.
She knitted blue angora trees.
She purl stitched countless purple fleas.
She knitted a palace in need of a darn.
She knitted a battle and ran out of yarn.

She drew out a strand
Of her gleaming, green hair
And knitted a lawn
Till she just wasn't there.

KARLA KUSKIN

There Was an Old Woman

There was an old woman, as I've heard tell,
She went to the market, her eggs for to sell;
She went to market all on a market day,
And she fell asleep on the King's highway.

There came a pedlar, whose name was Stout,
He cut her petticoats all round about;
He cut her petticoats up to the knees,
Which made the old woman to shiver and freeze.

When the little woman first did wake,
She began to shiver and she began to shake,
She began to wonder and she began to cry,
"Oh! deary, deary me, this is none of I!"

"But if it be I, as I do hope it be,
I've a little dog at home and he'll know me;
If it be I, he'll wag his little tail,
And if it be not I, he'll loudly bark and wail."

Home went the little woman all in the dark,
Up got the little dog, and he began to bark;
He began to bark, so she began to cry,
"Oh, deary, deary me, this is none of I!"

MOTHER GOOSE

Miss M. F. H. E. I. I. Jones

Melissa Finnan Haddie
Eevy Ivy Ipswich Jones
Used to sit and sigh and cry
On solitary stones.
"No one, no one, no one
Will play with me," she said.
"I wish my name were
Lillian or Lindabelle instead
Of what it is.
For then you see
The others would not laugh at me
And point and snicker when I pass.
Oh, woe is me," said she,
"Alas."

Well, one day when Melissa
Was wandering through town
She chanced upon a baby
Who was just about to drown.
She took her shoes and stockings off
And jumping from the spot,
She dived right in
And soaked her skin
And saved the tiny tot.

Then everybody thanked her
And the children who were mean
Turned suddenly quite purple
And then at once pale green,
And they said to her,
"Melissa, please come and join our games.
You know," they said,
"You really have
A lovely set of names."

KARLA KUSKIN

Jim
Who ran away from his Nurse,
and was eaten by a Lion

There was a Boy whose name was Jim;
His Friends were very good to him.
They gave him Tea, and Cakes, and Jam,
And slices of delicious Ham,
And Chocolate with pink inside,
And little Tricycles to ride,
And read him Stories through and through,
And even took him to the Zoo—
But there it was the dreadful Fate
Befell him, which I now relate.

You know—at least you *ought* to know,
For I have often told you so—
That Children never are allowed
To leave their Nurses in a Crowd;
Now this was Jim's especial Foible,
He ran away when he was able,
And on this inauspicious day
He slipped his hand and ran away!
He hadn't gone a yard when—Bang!
With open Jaws, a Lion sprang,
And hungrily began to eat
The Boy: beginning at his feet.

Now, just imagine how it feels
When first your toes and then your heels,
And then by gradual degrees,
Your shins and ankles, calves and knees,
Are slowly eaten, bit by bit.
No wonder Jim detested it!
No wonder that he shouted "Hi!"
The Honest Keeper heard his cry,
Though very fat he almost ran
To help the little gentleman.
"Ponto!" he ordered as he came
(For Ponto was the Lion's name),
"Ponto!" he cried, with angry Frown.
"Let go, Sir! Down, Sir! Put it down!"

The Lion made a sudden Stop,
He let the Dainty Morsel drop,
And slunk reluctant to his Cage,
Snarling with Disappointed Rage.
But when he bent him over Jim,
The Honest Keeper's Eyes were dim.
The Lion having reached his Head,
The Miserable Boy was dead!
When Nurse informed his Parents, they
Were more Concerned than I can say:—
His Mother, as she dried her eyes,
Said, "Well—it gives me no surprise,
He would not do as he was told!"
His Father, who was self-controlled,
Bade all the children round attend
To James's miserable end,
And always keep a-hold of Nurse
For fear of finding something worse.

HILAIRE BELLOC

Pinky Pauper picked my pocket,
Took my darling's silver locket,
I caught him sleeping—eight, nine, ten—
And stole the locket back again.

CLYDE WATSON

Raccoon

One summer night a little Raccoon,
Above his left shoulder, looked at the new moon.
 He made a wish;
 He said: "I wish
 I were a Catfish,
 A Blowfish, a Squid,
 A Katydid,
 A Beetle, a Skink,
 An Ostrich, a pink
 Flamingo, a Gander,
 A Salamander,
 A Hippopotamus,
 A Duck-billed Platypus,
 A Gecko, a Slug,
 A Water Bug,
 A pug-nosed Beaver,
 Anything whatever
Except what I am, a little Raccoon!"

Above his left shoulder, the Evening Star
Listened and heard the little Raccoon
 Who wished on the moon;
 And she said: "Why wish
 You were a Catfish,
 A Blowfish, a Squid,
 A Katydid,
 A Beetle, a Skink,

An Ostrich, a pink
Flamingo, a Gander,
A Salamander,
A Hippopotamus,
A Duck-billed Platypus,
A Gecko, a Slug,
A Water Bug,
A pug-nosed Beaver,
Anything whatever?
Why must you change?" said the Evening Star,
"When you are perfect as you are?
I know a boy who wished on the moon
That *he* might be a little Raccoon!"

WILLIAM JAY SMITH

The Black Pebble

There went three children down to the shore,
    Down to the shore and back;
There was skipping Susan and bright-eyed Sam
    And little scowling Jack.

Susan found a white cockle-shell,
    The prettiest ever seen,
And Sam picked up a piece of glass
    Rounded and smooth and green.

143

But Jack found only a plain black pebble
   That lay by the rolling sea,
And that was all that ever he found;
   So back they went all three.

The cockle-shell they put on the table,
   The green glass on the shelf,
But the little black pebble that Jack had found,
   He kept it for himself.

JAMES REEVES

Mary lost her coat,
Mary lost her hat,
Mary lost her fifty cents—
Now what do you think of that?

Mary *found* her coat,
Mary *found* her hat,
Mary *found* her fifty cents—
Now what do you think of *that*?

FOLK RHYME

Mumps

I had a feeling in my neck,
And on the sides were two big bumps;
I couldn't swallow anything
At all because I had the mumps.

And Mother tied it with a piece,
And then she tied up Will and John,
And no one else but Dick was left
That didn't have a mump rag on.

He teased at us and laughed at us,
And said, whenever he went by,
"It's vinegar and lemon drops
And pickles!" just to make us cry.

But Tuesday Dick was very sad
And cried because his neck was sore,
And not a one said sour things
To anybody any more.

ELIZABETH MADOX ROBERTS

The fly made a visit to the grocery store
Didn't even knock—went right in the door.
He took a bite of sugar, and took a bite of ham,
Then he sat down to rest on the grocery man.

FOLK RHYME

145

A Pig Tale

Poor Jane Higgins,
   She had five piggins,
And one got drowned in the Irish Sea.
   Poor Jane Higgins,
   She had four piggins,
And one flew over a sycamore tree.
   Poor Jane Higgins,
   She had three piggins,
And one was taken away for pork.
   Poor Jane Higgins,
   She had two piggins,
And one was sent to the Bishop of Cork.
   Poor Jane Higgins,
   She had one piggin,
And that was struck by a shower of hail,
   So poor Jane Higgins,
   She had no piggins,
And that's the end of my little pig tale.

JAMES REEVES

Repetitions
Variations

Beautiful Soup

Beautiful Soup, so rich and green,
Waiting in a hot tureen!
Who for such dainties would not stoop?
Soup of the evening, beautiful Soup!
Soup of the evening, beautiful Soup!
    Beau—ootiful Soo—oop!
    Beau—ootiful Soo—oop!
Soo—oop of the e—e—evening,
    Beautiful, beautiful Soup!

Beautiful Soup! Who cares for fish,
Game, or any other dish?
Who would not give all else for two p
ennyworth only of beautiful Soup?
Pennyworth only of beautiful Soup?
    Beau—ootiful Soo—oop!
    Beau—ootiful Soo—oop!
Soo—oop of the e—e—evening,
    Beautiful, beauti—FUL SOUP!"

LEWIS CARROLL

The Song of Mr. Toad

The world has held great Heroes,
  As history books have showed;
But never a name to go down to fame
  Compared with that of Toad!

The clever men at Oxford
  Know all that there is to be knowed.
But they none of them know one half as much
  As intelligent Mr. Toad!

The animals sat in the Ark and cried,
  Their tears in torrents flowed.
Who was it said, "There's land ahead"?
  Encouraging Mr. Toad!

The Army all saluted
  As they marched along the road.
Was it the King? Or Kitchener?
  No. It was Mr. Toad!

The Queen and her Ladies-in-waiting
  Sat at the window and sewed.
She cried, "Look! who's that *handsome* man?"
  They answered, "Mr. Toad."

KENNETH GRAHAME

My Donkey

My donkey, my dear,
Had a pain in his head;
A kind lady gave him
A bonnet of red,
And little shoes of lavender,
Lav–lav–lavender,
And little shoes of lavender
To keep him from the cold.

My donkey, my dear,
Had a pain in his throat;
A kind lady gave him
A button-up coat,
And little shoes of lavender,
Lav–lav–lavender,
And little shoes of lavender
To keep him from the cold.

My donkey, my dear,
Had a pain in his chest;
A kind lady gave him
A thick woolly vest,
And little shoes of lavender,
Lav–lav–lavender,
And little shoes of lavender,
To keep him from the cold.

ROSE FYLEMAN

Quack!

The duck is whiter than whey is,
His tail tips up over his back,
The eye in his head is as round as a button,
And he says, *Quack! Quack!*

He swims on his bright blue mill-pond,
By the willow tree under the shack,
Then stands on his head to see down to the bottom,
And says, *Quack! Quack!*

When Mollie steps out of the kitchen,
For apron—pinned round with a sack;
He squints at her round face, her dish, and what's in it,
And says, *Quack! Quack!*

He preens the pure snow of his feathers
In the sun by the wheat-straw stack;
At dusk waddles home with his brothers and sisters,
And says, *Quack! Quack!*

WALTER DE LA MARE

The Mysterious Cat

I saw a proud, mysterious cat,
I saw a proud, mysterious cat
Too proud to catch a mouse or rat—
Mew, mew, mew.

But catnip she would eat, and purr,
But catnip she would eat, and purr,
And goldfish she did much prefer—
Mew, mew, mew.

I saw a cat—'twas but a dream,
I saw a cat—'twas but a dream
Who scorned the slave that brought her cream—
Mew, mew, mew.

Unless the slave were dressed in style,
Unless the slave were dressed in style
And knelt before her all the while—
Mew, mew, mew.

Did you ever hear of a thing like that?
Did you ever hear of a thing like that?
Did you ever hear of a thing like that?
Oh, what a proud mysterious cat.
Oh, what a proud mysterious cat.
Oh, what a proud mysterious cat.
Mew . . . mew . . . mew.

VACHEL LINDSAY

The Goblin

A goblin lives in *our* house, in *our* house, in *our* house,
A goblin lives in *our* house all the year round.
He bumps
And he jumps
And he thumps
And he stumps.
He knocks
And he rocks
And he rattles at the locks.

A goblin lives in *our* house, in *our* house, in *our* house,
A goblin lives in *our* house all the year round.

ROSE FYLEMAN

The wind has such a rainy sound
    Moaning through the town,
The sea has such a windy sound,—
    Will the ships go down?

The apples in the orchard
    Tumble from their tree.—
Oh will the ships go down, go down,
    In the windy sea?

CHRISTINA ROSSETTI

Old Snake Has Gone to Sleep

Sun shining bright on the mountain rock
Old snake has gone to sleep.
Wild flowers blooming round the mountain rock
Old snake has gone to sleep.
Bees buzzing near the mountain rock
Old snake has gone to sleep.
Sun shining warm on the mountain rock
Old snake has gone to sleep.

MARGARET WISE BROWN

The Mock Turtle's Song

"Will you walk a little faster?" said a whiting to a snail.
"There's a porpoise close behind us, and he's treading on
    my tail.
See how eagerly the lobsters and the turtles all advance!
They are waiting on the shingle—will you come and join
    the dance?
    Will you, won't you, will you, won't you, will you
        join the dance?
    Will you, won't you, will you, won't you, won't you
        join the dance?

'You can really have no notion how delightful it will be,
When they take us up and throw us, with the lobsters,
      out to sea!"
But the snail replied "Too far, too far!" and gave a look
      askance—
Said he thanked the whiting kindly, but he would not
      join the dance.
   Would not, could not, would not, could not, would
      not join the dance.
   Would not, could not, would not, could not, could not
      join the dance.

"What matters it how far we go?" his scaly friend replied.
"There is another shore, you know, upon the other side.
The further off from England the nearer is to France—
Then turn not pale, beloved snail, but come and join the
      dance.
   Will you, won't you, will you, won't you, will you join
      the dance?
   Will you, won't you, will you, won't you, won't you
      join the dance?"

LEWIS CARROLL

Teapots and Quails

Teapots and Quails,
Snuffers and snails,
Set him a sailing
and see how he sails!

Mitres and beams,
Thimbles and Creams,
Set him a screaming
and hark! how he screams!

Ribands and Pigs,
Helmets and Figs,
Set him a jigging
and see how he jigs!

Tadpoles and Tops,
Teacups and Mops,
Set him a hopping
and see how he hops!

Lobsters and owls,
Scissors and fowls,
Set him a howling
and hark how he howls!

Eagles and pears,
Slippers and Bears,
Set him a staring
and see how he stares!

Sofas and bees,
Camels and Keys,
Set him a sneezing
and see how he'll sneeze!

Thistles and Moles,
Crumpets and Soles,
Set it a rolling
and see how it rolls!

Hurdles and Mumps,
Poodles and pumps,
Set it a jumping
and see how he jumps!

Pancakes and Fins,
Roses and Pins,
Set him a grinning
and see how he grins!

EDWARD LEAR

The Leaves Fall Down

One by one the leaves fall down
From the sky come falling one by one
And leaf by leaf the summer is done
One by one by one by one.

MARGARET WISE BROWN

Neuteronomy

The elevator stops at every floor
and nobody opens and closes the door,
and nobody talks to his neighbor anymore
where the neuter computer goes *tick,*
where the neuter computer goes *click.*

You call the operator on the telephone
and say Help! I'm in trouble and I'm here all alone!
and all you get back is a phoney dial tone
where the neuter computer goes *clank,*
where the neuter computer goes *blank.*

There's no more teacher to be nice or mean
when you learn your lessons from a teaching machine
and plug in your prayers to the preaching machine
where the neuter computer goes *bless,*
where the neuter computer noes *yes.*

From when you are born until you are old
the facts of your life are all controlled,
put your dreams on a punch card—don't staple or fold
where the neuter computer prints *file,*
where the neuter computer prints *smile.*

There's no one to love and no one to hate,
and no more misfortune or chance or fate
in this automated obligated zero perfect state
where the neuter computer goes *think,*

where the neuter computer goes *blink*
   blink think blink think blink blink blink
    blinkthink
    thinkblink
     blink
      think
       blink

EVE MERRIAM

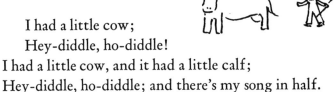

I had a little cow;
  Hey-diddle, ho-diddle!
I had a little cow, and it had a little calf;
Hey-diddle, ho-diddle; and there's my song in half.

  I had a little cow;
  Hey-diddle, ho-diddle!
I had a little cow, and I drove it to the stall;
Hey-diddle, ho-diddle; and there's my song all!

MOTHER GOOSE

I went to the river
And couldn't get across,
Paid five dollars
For an old gray hoss.

The horse wouldn't pull,
So I traded for a bull;

The bull wouldn't holler,
So I traded for a dollar;

The dollar wouldn't pass,
So I throwed it in the grass;

The grass wouldn't grow,
So I traded for a hoe;

The hoe wouldn't dig,
So I traded for a pig;

The pig wouldn't squeal,
So I traded for a wheel;

The wheel wouldn't run,
So I traded for a gun;

The gun wouldn't shoot,
So I traded for a boot;

The boot wouldn't fit,
So I thought I'd better quit.

FOLK RHYME

What the Gray Cat Sings

The Cat was once a weaver,
  A weaver, a weaver,
An old and withered weaver
  Who labored late and long;
And while she made the shuttle hum
And wove the weft and clipped the thrum,
Beside the loom with droning drum
  She sang the weaving song:
    "Pr-rrum, pr-rrum,
Thr-ree thr-reads in the thr-rum,
    Pr-rrum!"

The Cat's no more a weaver,
  A weaver, a weaver,
An old and wrinkled weaver,
  For though she did no wrong,
A witch hath changed the shape of her
That dwindled down and clothed in fur
Beside the hearth with droning purr
  She thrums her weaving song:
    "Pr-rrum, pr-rrum,
Thr-ree thr-reads in the thr-rum,
    Pr-rrum!"

ARTHUR GUITERMAN

161

Two cats were sitting in a tree,
kritte vitte vit bom bom,
a cat called Lew,
a cat called Lee,
kritte vitte vit bom bom.
"Now follow me,"
said Lew to Lee,
kritte vitte vitte vitte vit bom bom,
"for I no longer like this tree,"
kritte vitte vit bom bom!

So Lew and Lee
climbed down the tree,
kritte vitte vit bom bom.
Once down the tree
to Lew said Lee,
kritte vitte vit bom bom,
"Oh, Lew I rather liked that tree!"
kritte vitte vitte vitte vit bom bom.
So Lew and Lee climbed up the tree,
Kritte vitte vit bom bom!

N. M. BODECKER

162

If all the seas were one sea,
What a great sea that would be!
And if all the trees were one tree,
What a great tree that would be!
And if all the axes were one axe,
What a great axe that would be!
And if all men were one man,
What a great man he would be!
And if the great man took the great axe,
And cut down the great tree,
And let it fall into the great sea,
What a splish-splash that would be!

MOTHER GOOSE

To See the Rabbit

We are going to see the rabbit.
We are going to see the rabbit.
Which rabbit, people say?
Which rabbit, ask the children?
Which rabbit?
The only rabbit,
The only rabbit in England,
Sitting behind a barbed-wire fence
Under the floodlights, neon lights,
Sodium lights,

Nibbling grass
On the only patch of grass
In England, in England
(Except the grass by the hoardings
Which doesn't count).
We are going to see the rabbit
And we must be there on time.

First we shall go by escalator,
Then we shall go by underground,
And then we shall go by motorway,
And then by helicopterway,
And the last ten yards we shall have to go
On foot.

And now we are going
All the way to see the rabbit,
We are nearly there,
We are longing to see it,
And so is the crowd
Which is here in thousands
With mounted policemen
And big loudspeakers
And bands and banners,
And everyone has come a long way.
But soon we shall see it
Sitting and nibbling
The blades of grass
On the only patch of grass
In—but something has gone wrong!

Why is everyone so angry,
Why is everyone jostling
And slanging and complaining?

The rabbit has gone,
Yes, the rabbit has gone.
He has actually burrowed down into the earth
And made himself a warren, under the earth,
Despite all these people.
And what shall we do?
What *can* we do?
It is all a pity, you must be disappointed,
Go home and do something else for today,
Go home again, go home for today.
For you cannot hear the rabbit, under the earth,
Remarking rather sadly to himself, by himself,
As he rests in his warren, under the earth:
"It won't be long, they are bound to come,
They are bound to come and find me, even here."

ALAN BROWNJOHN

Names
from Prologue to
THE FAMILY OF MAN

There is only one horse on the earth
and his name is All Horses.
There is only one bird in the air
and his name is All Wings.
There is only one fish in the sea
and his name is All Fins.
There is only one man in the world
and his name is All Men.
There is only one woman in the world
and her name is All Women.
There is only one child in the world
and the child's name is All Children.
  There is only one Maker in the world
  and His children cover the earth
  and they are named All God's Children.

CARL SANDBURG

The Ceremonial Band
(*To be said out loud by a chorus and solo voices*)

The old King of Dorchester,
He had a little orchestra,
And never did you hear such a ceremonial band.
"Tootle-too," said the flute,
"Deed-a-reedle," said the fiddle,
For the fiddles and the flutes were the finest in the land.

The old King of Dorchester,
He had a little orchestra,
And never did you hear such a ceremonial band.
"Pump-a-rum," said the drum,
"Tootle-too," said the flute,
"Deed-a-reedle," said the fiddle,
For the fiddles and the flutes were the finest in the land.

The old King of Dorchester,
He had a little orchestra,
And never did you hear such a ceremonial band.
"Pickle-pee," said the fife,
"Pump-a-rum," said the drum,
"Tootle-too," said the flute,
"Deed-a-reedle," said the fiddle,
For the fiddles and the flutes were the finest in the land.

The old King of Dorchester,
He had a little orchestra,
And never did you hear such a ceremonial band.

167

"Zoomba-zoom," said the bass,
"Pickle-pee," said the fife,
"Pump-a-rum," said the drum,
"Tootle-too," said the flute,
"Deed-a-reedle," said the fiddle,
For the fiddles and the flutes were the finest in the land.

The old King of Dorchester,
He had a little orchestra,
And never did you hear such a ceremonial band.
"Pah-pa-rah," said the trumpet,
"Zoomba-zoom," said the bass,
"Pickle-pee," said the fife,
"Pump-a-rum," said the drum.
"Tootle-too," said the flute,
"Deed-a-reedle," said the fiddle,
For the fiddles and the flutes were the finest in the land,
Oh! the fiddles and the flutes were the finest in the land!

JAMES REEVES

Lingual Gyrations

Bibbilibonty

On the Bibbilibonty hill
Stands a Bibbilibonty house;
In the Bibbilibonty house
Are Bibbilibonty people;
The Bibbilibonty people
Have Bibbilibonty children;
And the Bibbilibonty children
Take a Bibbilibonty sup
With a Bibbilibonty spoon
From a Bibbilibonty cup.

ROSE FYLEMAN

Marty's Party

Marty's party?
Jamie came. He
seemed to Judy
dreadful rude. He
joggled Davy,
spilled his gravy,
squeezed a melon
seed at Helen,
gave a poke so
Eddy's Coke so

fresh and fizzy
showered Lizzy;
jostled Frank who
dropped a hank
of juicy candy.
Debby handy—
double bubble
gum in trouble—
Debbie mebbie
stumbled, bumbled
into Jessie.
Very messy!
Very sticky!

That's a quickie—
not so ludi-
crous to Judy,
watching Jamie
jilting Amy,
wilting Mamie,
finding Vicky.

What a tricky
lad! Where's Marty?
Don't know. She just
gave the party.

DAVID MCCORD

For wandering walks
In the sparkling snow
No one is muffled
More warmly than Joe.
No one is mittened more
Coated or hatted
Booted or sweatered,
Both knitted and tatted,
Buttoned and zippered
Tied, tucked and belted
Padded and wadded
And quilted and felted,
Hooked in and hooded,
Tweeded and twilled.
Nothing of Joe's
From his top to his toes
But the tip of his nose
Could be touched
By the snows
Or the wind as it blows,
And grow rather rosy
The way a nose grows
If it's frozen
Or possibly chilled.

KARLA KUSKIN

The Pickety Fence

The pickety fence
The pickety fence
Give it a lick it's
The pickety fence
Give it a lick it's
A clickety fence
Give it a lick it's
A lickety fence
Give it a lick
Give it a lick
Give it a lick
With a rickety stick
Pickety
Pickety
Pickety
Pick

DAVID MCCORD

Auk Talk

The raucous auk must squawk to talk.
The squawk auks squawk to talk goes
AUK.

MARY ANN HOBERMAN

173

I Had a Hippopotamus

I had a hippopotamus; I kept him in a shed
And fed him upon vitamins and vegetable bread;
I made him my companion on many cheery walks
And had his portrait done by a celebrity in chalks.

His charming eccentricities were known on every side,
The creature's popularity was wonderfully wide;
He frolicked with the Rector in a dozen friendly tussles,
Who could not but remark upon his hippopotamuscles.

If he should be afflicted by depression or the dumps,
By hippopotameasles or the hippopotamumps,
I never knew a particle of peace till it was plain
He was hippopotamasticating properly again.

I had a hippopotamus; I loved him as a friend;
But beautiful relationships are bound to have an end.
Time takes, alas! our joys from us and robs us of our blisses;
My hippopotamus turned out a hippopotamissis.

My housekeeper regarded him with jaundice in her eye;
She did not want a colony of hippopotami;
She borrowed a machine-gun from her soldier-nephew,
    Percy,
And showed my hippopotamus no hippopotamercy.

My house now lacks the glamour that the charming
    creature gave,

The garage where I kept him is as silent as the grave;
No longer he displays among the motor-tyres and spanners
His hippopotamastery of hippopotamanners.

No longer now he gambols in the orchard in the Spring;
No longer do I lead him through the village on a string;
No longer in the mornings does the neighbourhood rejoice
To his hippopotamusically-modulated voice.

I had a hippopotamus; but nothing upon earth
Is constant in its happiness or lasting in its mirth.
No joy that life can give me can be strong enough to
    smother
My sorrow for that might-have-been-a-hippopota-mother.

PATRIC BARRINGTON

Circles

The thing to draw with compasses
Are suns and moons and circleses
And rows of humptydumpasses
Or anything in circuses
Like hippopotamusseses
And hoops and camels' humpasses
And wheels on clownses busseses
And fat old elephumpasses.

HARRY BEHN

The Yak

Yickity-yackity, yickity-yak,
the yak has a scriffily, scraffily back;
some yaks are brown yaks and some yaks are black,
yickity-yackity, yickity-yak.

Sniggildy-snaggildy, sniggildy-snag,
the yak is all covered with shiggildy-shag;
he walks with a ziggildy-zaggildy-zag,
sniggildy-snaggildy, sniggildy-snag.

Yickity-yackity, yickity-yak,
the yak has a scriffily, scraffily back;
some yaks are brown yaks and some yaks are black,
yickity-yackity, yickity-yak.

JACK PRELUTSKY

The Tutor

A tutor who tooted the flute
Tried to teach two young tooters to toot.
Said the two to the tutor,
"Is it harder to toot or
To tutor two tooters to toot?"

CAROLYN WELLS

Don't Ever Seize a Weasel by the Tail

You should never squeeze a weasel
for you might displease the weasel,
and don't ever seize a weasel by the tail.

Let his tail blow in the breeze;
if you pull it, he will sneeze,
for the weasel's constitution tends to be a little frail.

Yes the weasel wheezes easily;
the weasel freezes easily;
the weasel's tan complexion rather suddenly turns pale.

So don't displease or tease a weasel,
squeeze or freeze or wheeze a weasel
and don't ever seize a weasel by the tail.

JACK PRELUTSKY

Gazelle

O gaze on the graceful gazelle as it grazes
It grazes on green growing leaves and on grasses
On grasses it grazes, go gaze as it passes
It passes so gracefully, gently, O gaze!

MARY ANN HOBERMAN

Tongue Twister

Someday I'll go to Winnipeg
To win a peg-leg pig.
But will a peg-leg winner win
The piglet's ill-got wig?

Someday I'll go to Ottawa
To eat a wall-eyed eel.
But ought a wall-eyed eater
Pot an eel that isn't peeled?

Someday I'll go to Nipigon
To nip a goony loon.
But will a goony nipper lose
His loony nipping spoon?

DENNIS LEE

Eletelephony

Once there was an elephant,
Who tried to use the telephant—
No! no! I mean an elephone
Who tried to use the telephone—
(Dear me! I am not certain quite
That even now I've got it right.)

178

Howe'er it was, he got his trunk
Entangled in the telephunk;
The more he tried to get it free
The louder buzzed the telephee—
(I fear I'd better drop the song
Of elephop and telephong!)

LAURA E. RICHARDS

Thistles

Thirty thirsty thistles
Thicketed and green
Growing in a grassy swamp
Purple-topped and lean
Prickily and thistley
Topped by tufts of thorns
Green mean little leaves on them
And tiny purple horns
Briary and brambley
A spikey, spiney bunch of them.
A troop of bright-red birds came by
And had a lovely lunch of them.

KARLA KUSKIN

Schenectady

Although I've been to Kankakee
And Kalamazoo and Kokomo,
The place I've always wanted to go,
The city I've always wanted to see
Is Schenectady.

Schenectady, Schenectady,
Though it's hard to pronounce correctly,
I plan to go there directly.

Schenectady, Schenectady,
Yes, I want to connect with Schenectady,
The town I select is Schenectady,
I elect to go to Schenectady,
I'll take any trek to Schenectady,
Even wash my neck for Schenectady,
So expect me next at Schenectady,
Check and double check
Schenectady!

EVE MERRIAM

Worm

squiggly wiggly wriggly jiggly higgly piggly worm
watch it wiggle   watch it wriggle   see it squiggle
    see it squirm

MARY ANN HOBERMAN

Charms
Chants
Incantations

Spring

I'm shouting
I'm singing
I'm swinging through trees
I'm winging skyhigh
With the buzzing black bees.
I'm the sun
I'm the moon
I'm the dew on the rose.
I'm a rabbit
Whose habit
Is twitching his nose.
I'm lively
I'm lovely
I'm kicking my heels.
I'm crying "Come dance"
To the fresh water eels.
I'm racing through meadows
Without any coat
I'm a gamboling lamb
I'm a light leaping goat
I'm a bud
I'm a bloom
I'm a dove on the wing.
I'm running on rooftops
And welcoming spring!

KARLA KUSKIN

The High Skip,
The Sly Skip,
The Skip like a Feather,
The Long Skip,
The Strong Skip,
And the Skip All Together!

The Slow Skip,
The Toe Skip,
The Skip Double-Double,
The Fast Skip,
The Last Skip,
And the Skip Against Trouble!

ELEANOR FARJEON

Over and Under

Bridges are for going over water,
Boats are for going over sea;
Dots are for going over dotted *i*'s,
And blankets are for going over me.

Over and under,
Over and under,
Crack the whip,
And hear the thunder.

Divers are for going under water,
Seals are for going under sea;
Fish are for going under mermaid's eyes,
And pillows are for going under me.

Over and under,
Over and under,
Crack the whip,
And hear the thunder,
Crack-crack-crack,
Hear the crack of thunder!

WILLIAM JAY SMITH

Rattlesnake Skipping Song

Mississauga rattlesnakes
Eat brown bread.
Mississauga rattlesnakes
Fall down dead.
If you catch a caterpillar
Feed him apple juice;
But if you catch a rattlesnake
Turn him loose!

DENNIS LEE

This Is the Key

This is the Key of the Kingdom:
In that Kingdom is a city;
In that city is a town;
In that town there is a street;
In that street there winds a lane;
In that lane there is a yard;
In that yard there is a house;
In that house there waits a room;
In that room an empty bed;
And on that bed a basket—
A Basket of Sweet Flowers:
   Of Flowers, of Flowers;
   A Basket of Sweet Flowers.

Flowers in a Basket;
Basket on the bed;
Bed in the chamber;
Chamber in the house;
House in the weedy yard;
Yard in the winding lane;
Lane in the broad street;
Street in the high town;
Town in the city;
City in the Kingdom—
This is the Key of the Kingdom.
   Of the Kingdom this is the Key.

MOTHER GOOSE

Pick Me Up

Pick me up with a pile of blocks
And carry me past the Cuckoo Clocks!

Pick me up with a pile of hay
And carry me off to Buzzards Bay!

Pick me up with a pile of snow
And carry me out to Idaho!

Pick me up with a pile of twine
And carry me down to the Argentine!

Pick me up with a pile of lava
And carry me over the hills of Java!

Pick me up with a pile of sand
And put me down in Newfoundland!

WILLIAM JAY SMITH

Alligator Pie

Alligator pie, alligator pie,
If I don't get some I think I'm gonna die.
Give away the green grass, give away the sky,
But don't give away my alligator pie.

186

Alligator stew, alligator stew,
If I don't get some I don't know what I'll do.
Give away my furry hat, give away my shoe,
But don't give away my alligator stew.

Alligator soup, alligator soup,
If I don't get some I think I'm gonna droop.
Give away my hockey-stick, give away my hoop,
But don't give away my alligator soup.

DENNIS LEE

The Crossing of Mary of Scotland

Mary, Mary, Queen of Scots,
Dressed in yellow polka dots,
Sailed one rainy winter day,
Sailed from Dover to Calais,
Sailed in tears, heart tied in knots;
Face broke out in scarlet spots
The size of yellow polka dots—
Forgot to take her *booster* shots,
Queen of Scotland, Queen of Scots!

WILLIAM JAY SMITH

Row, row, row
to Oyster Bay.
What sort of fish
shall we catch today?
Big fish,
small fish,
snook or snail,
yellow snapper,
triple tail,
herring
daring,
kipper
coarse,
or a trout
with applesauce?

N. M. BODECKER

Catching-Song
A Play-Rhyme
(*For any number of Players*)

You can't catch *me*!
You can't catch *me*!
Run as swift as quicksilver,
You can't catch *me*!

If you can catch me you shall have a ball
That once the daughter of a king let fall;
It ran down the hill and it rolled on the plain,
And the king's daughter never caught her ball again,

    And you can't catch *me*!
    You can't catch *me*!
    Run as quick as lightning,
    But you can't catch *me*!

If you can catch me you shall have a bird
That once the son of a beggar heard.
He climbed up the tree, but the bird flew away,
And the beggar's son never caught a bird that day,

    And you can't catch *me*!
    You can't catch *me*!
    Run as fast as water,
    But you can't catch *me*!

ELEANOR FARJEON

How many miles to Old Norfolk
To see a magician breathe fire & smoke?
    One, two, three, four,
    Only three miles more.
How many miles to Christmas Cove
To eat of an applecake baked with clove?
    One, two, three, four,
    Only two miles more.
How many miles to Newburyport
For trinkets & sweets of every sort?
    One, two, three, four,
    Only one mile more.
How many miles to Lavender Spring
To hear a fine trumpeter play for the King?
    One, two, three, four,
    Here we are, we'll go no more.

CLYDE WATSON

Songs
Dirges
Lamentations

Who Is Sad?

Who is sad and who is sorry?
Not the seagull flying high,
not the wren, brown as earth is,
not the bumblebee buzzing by,
not the cat upon the doorstep,
not the dog beside the gate—
they are neither sad nor sorry,
proud, ashamed, on time, nor late.

ELIZABETH COATSWORTH

Ariel's Dirge

Full fathom five thy father lies;
  Of his bones are coral made;
Those are pearls that were his eyes;
Nothing of him that doth fade
But doth suffer a sea-change
Into something rich and strange.
Sea-nymphs hourly ring his knell:
                    Ding-dong.
Hark! now I hear them,—Ding-dong, bell.

WILLIAM SHAKESPEARE

Spring

The last snow is going,
Brooks are overflowing,
A sunny wind is blowing
    Swiftly along.

Through sky birds are blowing,
On earth green is showing,
You can feel earth growing
    Quiet and strong.

A sunny wind is blowing,
Farmer's busy sowing,
Apple trees are snowing,
    And shadows grow long.

Now the wind is slowing,
Cows begin lowing,
Evening clouds are glowing
    And dusk is full of song.

HARRY BEHN

I Had a Little Pony

I had a little pony,
His name was Dapple Gray;
I lent him to a lady
To ride a mile away.

She whipped him, she lashed him,
She rode him through the mire;
I would not lend my pony now
For all that lady's hire.

MOTHER GOOSE

An Epitaph

Here lies a most beautiful lady,
Light of step and heart was she;
I think she was the most beautiful lady
That ever was in the West Country.

But beauty vanishes; beauty passes;
However rare—rare it be;
And when I crumble, who will remember
This lady of the West Country?

WALTER DE LA MARE

Gone

Where's the Queen of Sheba?
Where King Solomon?
Gone with Boy Blue who looks after the sheep,
Gone and gone and gone.

Lovely is the sunshine;
Lovely is the wheat;
Lovely the wind from out of the clouds
Having its way with it.

Rise up, Old Green-Stalks!
Delve deep, Old Corn!
But where's the Queen of Sheba?
Where King Solomon?

WALTER DE LA MARE

All that is gold does not glitter,
    Not all those who wander are lost;
The old that is strong does not wither,
    Deep roots are not reached by the frost.
From the ashes a fire shall be woken,
    A light from the shadows shall spring;
Renewed shall be blade that was broken:
    The crownless again shall be king.

J. R. R. TOLKIEN

Four Little Foxes

Speak gently, Spring, and make no sudden sound;
For in my windy valley, yesterday, I found
New-born foxes squirming on the ground—
    Speak gently.

Walk softly, March, forbear the bitter blow;
Her feet within a trap, her blood upon the snow,
The four little foxes saw their mother go—
    Walk softly.

Go lightly, Spring, oh, give them no alarm;
When I covered them with boughs to shelter them from
      harm,
The thin blue foxes suckled at my arm—
    Go lightly.

Step softly, March, with your rampant hurricane;
Nuzzling one another, and whimpering with pain,
The new little foxes are shivering in the rain—
    Step softly.

LEW SARETT

196

Small Dirge

Small comfort the candle
Of moon on the maple,
The steeple of poplar,
The arch of the birch.

Small comfort the yellow
Of sun on the linden.
Small comfort the ripple
Of wind in the larch.

Small comfort the shadow
Of ash and of alder,
Of elm and of willow
Now that you lie

Where comfort is hollow
And hope is shallow
With dust for your pillow
And dust for your sky.

ISABEL WILNER

197

A Dirge for a Righteous Kitten

*(To be intoned, all but the two italicized lines, which
are to be spoken in a snappy, matter-of-fact way)*

Ding-dong, ding-dong, ding-dong.
Here lies a kitten good, who kept
A kitten's proper place.
He stole no pantry eatables,
Nor scratched the baby's face.
He let the alley-cats alone.
He had no yowling vice.
His shirt was always laundried well,
He freed the house of mice.
Until his death he had not caused
His little mistress tears,
He wore his ribbon prettily,
He washed behind his ears.
Ding-dong, ding-dong, ding-dong.

VACHEL LINDSAY

Admonitions
Exhortations

Hurt No Living Thing

Hurt no living thing,
Ladybird nor butterfly,
Nor moth with dusty wing,
Nor cricket chirping cheerily,
Nor grasshopper, so light of leap,
Nor dancing gnat,
Nor beetle fat,
Nor harmless worms that creep.

CHRISTINA ROSSETTI

The Snake

Don't ever make
the bad mistake
of stepping on
the sleeping snake

because
his jaws

might be awake.

JACK PRELUTSKY

Rules

Do not jump on ancient uncles.
Do not yell at average mice.
Do not wear a broom to breakfast.
Do not ask a snake's advice.
Do not bathe in chocolate pudding.
Do not talk to bearded bears.
Do not smoke cigars on sofas.
Do not dance on velvet chairs.
Do not take a whale to visit
Russell's mother's cousin's yacht.
And whatever else you do do
It is better you
Do not.

KARLA KUSKIN

I Stole Brass

Policeman, policeman, don't take me,
Take that man behind that tree;
I stole brass, he stole gold—
Policeman, policeman, don't take hold!

FOLK RHYME

My Mother Said

My mother said, I never should
Play with the gipsies in the wood.

If I did, she would say,
"You naughty girl to disobey.

"Your hair shan't curl and your shoes shan't shine;
You gipsy girl, you shan't be mine."

And my father said that if I did
He'd rap my head with the teapot-lid.

NURSERY RHYME

Sea Gull

The sea gull curves his wings,
the sea gull turns his eyes.
Get down into the water, fish!
(if you are wise.)

The sea gull slants his wings,
the sea gull turns his head.
Get deep into the water, fish!
(or you'll be dead.)

ELIZABETH COATSWORTH

If You Ever

If you ever ever ever ever ever
    If you ever ever ever meet a whale
You must never never never never never
    You must never never never touch its tail:
For if you ever ever ever ever ever,
    If you ever ever ever touch its tail,
You will never never never never never,
    You will never never meet another whale.

ANONYMOUS

Little Martha piggy-wig
Run away and dance a jig!
If you weren't so fat and sweet
You wouldn't be so good to eat.

CLYDE WATSON

We Must Be Polite
(Lessons for children on how to behave under peculiar circumstances)

1

If we meet a gorilla
what shall we do?
Two things we may do
if we so wish to do.

Speak to the gorilla,
very, very respectfully,
"How do you do, sir?"

Or, speak to him with less
distinction of manner,
"Hey, why don't you go back
where you came from?"

2

If an elephant knocks on your door
and asks for something to eat,
there are two things to say:

Tell him there are nothing but cold
victuals in the house and he will do
better next door.

Or say: We have nothing but six bushels
of potatoes—will that be enough for
your breakfast, sir?

CARL SANDBURG

Little Girl, Be Careful What You Say

Little girl, be careful what you say
when you make talk with words, words—
for words are made of syllables
and syllables, child, are made of air—
and air is so thin—air is the breath of God—
air is finer than fire or mist,
finer than water or moonlight,
finer than spider-webs in the moon,
finer than water-flowers in the morning:
    and words are strong, too,
    stronger than rocks or steel
stronger than potatoes, corn, fish, cattle,
and soft, too, soft as little pigeon-eggs,
soft as the music of hummingbird wings.
    So, little girl, when you speak greetings,
when you tell jokes, make wishes or prayers,
    be careful, be careless, be careful,
    be what you wish to be.

CARL SANDBURG

For want of a nail, the shoe was lost,
For want of a shoe, the horse was lost,
For want of a horse, the rider was lost,
For want of a rider, the battle was lost,
For want of a battle, the kingdom was lost,
And all for the want of a horseshoe nail.

MOTHER GOOSE

For every evil under the sun
There is a remedy, or there is none.
If there be one, try and find it.
If there be none, never mind it.

NURSERY RHYME

Exclamations

Sally over the water,
Sally over the sea,
Sally broke a milk bottle
And blamed it on me.
I told Ma,
Ma told Pa,
Sally got a scolding,
Ha, ha, ha.

FOLK RHYME

Our Washing Machine

Our washing machine went whisity whirr
Whisity whisity whisity whirr
One day at noon it went whisity click
Whisity whisity whisity click
Click grr click grr click grr click
    Call the repairman
    Fix it . . . Quick!

PATRICIA HUBBELL

Hush my baby, don't say a word,
Daddy'll buy you a mocking bird.

When that mocking bird won't sing,
Daddy'll buy you a diamond ring.

When that diamond ring turns to brass,
Daddy'll buy you a looking glass.

When that looking glass gets broke,
Daddy'll buy you a billy goat.

When that billy goat gets bony,
Daddy'll buy you a shetland pony.

When that pony runs away,
Ta-ra-ra-ra-boom-de-ay.

FOLK RHYME

Alarm Clock

in the deep sleep forest
there were ferns
there were feathers
there was fur
and a soft ripe peach
on a branch within my

r-r-r-r-r-r-r-r-r-r-r-r-r-r-r-r-r-r-r-r-r-r-r-r-r-r-r

EVE MERRIAM

Goodness! Gracious! Have you heard the news?
The geese are going barefoot because they have
    no shoes.
When the cobbler finds his last and when he gets
    some leather
The geese need not go barefoot in all this bitter
    weather.

FOLK RHYME

I Woke Up This Morning

I woke up this morning
At quarter past seven.
I kicked up the covers
And stuck out my toe.
And ever since then
(That's a quarter past seven)
They haven't said anything
Other than "no."
They haven't said anything
Other than "Please, dear,
Don't do what you're doing."
Or "Lower your voice."
Whatever I've done
And however I've chosen,
I've done the wrong thing
And I've made the wrong choice.
I didn't wash well

And I didn't say thank you.
I didn't shake hands
And I didn't say please.
I didn't say sorry
When passing the candy.
I banged the box into
Miss Witelson's knees.
I didn't say sorry.
I didn't stand straighter.
I didn't speak louder
When asked what I'd said.
Well, I said
That tomorrow
At quarter past seven
They can
Come in and get me.
I'm Staying In Bed.

KARLA KUSKIN

Who's In?

"The door is shut fast
And everyone's out."
But people don't know
What they're talking about!
Says the fly on the wall,
And the flame on the coals,
And the dog on his rug,
And the mice in their holes,
And the kitten curled up,
And the spiders that spin—
"What, everyone out?
Why, everyone's in!"

ELIZABETH FLEMING

Hist Whist

hist   whist
little ghostthings
tip-toe
twinkle-toe

little twitchy
witches and tingling
goblins
hob-a-nob   hob-a-nob

little hoppy happy
toad in tweeds
tweeds
little itchy mousies

with scuttling
eyes   rustle and run   and
hidehidehide
whisk

whisk   look out for the old woman
with the wart on her nose
what she'll do to yer
nobody knows

for she knows the devil   ooch
the devil   ouch
the devil
ach   the great

green
dancing
devil
devil

devil
devil

wheeEEE

E. E. CUMMINGS

At the Keyhole

"Grill me some bones," said the Cobbler,
   "Some bones, my pretty Sue;
I'm tired of my lonesome with heels and soles,
Springsides and uppers too;
A mouse in the wainscot is nibbling;
A wind in the keyhole drones;
And a sheet webbed over my candle, Susie—
   Grill me some bones!"

"Grill me some bones," said the Cobbler,
   "I sat at my tic-tac-to;
And a footstep came to my door and stopped,
And a hand groped to and fro;
And I peered up over my boot and last;
And my feet went cold as stones:—
I saw an eye at the keyhole, Susie!—
   Grill me some bones!"

WALTER DE LA MARE

214

Anonymous

I know a poem of six lines that no one knows
who wrote, except
            that the poet was Chinese and lived
centuries before the birth of
Christ. I said it aloud
            once to some children, and when I reached
the last line suddenly they
understood and together all went—
                "Ooo!"
imagine that poem, written
            by a poet truly
who is Anonymous, since
            in the strict corporeal sense
he hasn't existed for thousands of years—imagine his little
                poem traveling
without gas or even a single grease job
across centuries of space and a million
miles of time
            to me, who spoke it
softly aloud to a group of children who heard
and suddenly all together
            cried "Ooo!"

MARTIN STEINGESSER

Index of Authors

Index of Titles

Index of First Lines

221

223

Isabel Wilner spent her childhood in China and in the Philippines. She came to America to attend college, and graduated from William Smith College and Carnegie Library School.

After working as a children's librarian in Pittsburgh and New York, and as an army librarian in the Philippines and in Okinawa, she went to Baltimore, Maryland, to be librarian of the laboratory school at Towson State College. Except for a year during which she exchanged with a British librarian and worked near London, she has been at Towson ever since.